# THE GOLDEN YEARS

*The Duchess of Duke Street*
*Book Two*

# Mollie Hardwick

SAPERE
BOOKS

# THE GOLDEN YEARS

Published by Sapere Books.

24 Trafalgar Road, Ilkley, LS29 8HH

saperebooks.com

ISBN: 978-0-85495-349-3

# CHAPTER ONE

The return of Charlie Tyrrell, now Lord Haslemere, to permanent residence at the Bentinck Hotel commenced a period of stability in Louisa Trotter's life of a kind she had not known since leaving her parents' home to make her independent way in the world.

In the two years from mid-1900, it seemed to her — on the rare occasions when she thought about it — that she had gone through a range of experience which no other London woman of lower middle-class origins could have matched. From being an apprentice cook, under a *chef de cuisine* who had at first done his best to deter her from that trade on the grounds that women didn't make good cooks, she had become established as the best freelance cook in London. From working in the kitchens of people who employed her to do so, she now employed others to cook in her own kitchen, that of the Bentinck, of which she was the leaseholder.

She had reluctantly acquired a husband, Augustus Trotter, who had been practically forced upon her in order to facilitate a liaison with the Prince of Wales, which she had not really wanted, but hadn't had the discourtesy to refuse. When the prince had become King Edward VII and had released her, she had acquired the Bentinck, and not long after been glad of the excuse to get rid of the feckless, frustrated Augustus, she hoped for ever. And then, of all things, she'd remind herself with wonder and some distaste, she'd gone and had a baby by Charlie Tyrrell as a result of one romantic fling, altogether uncharacteristic of her.

Luckily — for work, not domesticity, was Louisa's almost only interest in life — Charlie had arranged for the baby to be taken off her hands immediately, to be brought up by a childless couple on his country estate. The infant had never known her, and she had scarcely known it. An occasional twinge of conscience pricked her, but only an occasional one. She wouldn't have made a good mother, she knew, and the poor little thing would get a far better bringing-up where it was than in a hotel in the heart of London's West End.

There had been an offer of marriage from Charlie, but Louisa had refused. He was a lord. She was a coarse-grained career woman. She knew it could never have worked, but at least he had done the decent thing by making the gesture.

In fact, there had been no more romantic passages between them. It had been a single, unexpected escapade that had left no regrets on either side. He maintained his set of rooms in the Bentinck, living in them when he was in London and referring to them as 'home'. He went about town as much as ever, enjoying the bachelorhood which duty to his family line must someday inevitably terminate. He entertained women of his own class, mostly other men's wives, in his rooms, and Louisa cooked for them. She felt no jealousy. What he did with his life was none of her affair, but she was always glad to have him on the premises: a cheerful, affectionate, handsome friend.

So, with all these intrusions passed over, she had been able to settle down to her avowed task of making the Bentinck the best hotel in London. It wasn't the biggest by far. It wasn't the grandest. But an extensive word of mouth had it that it was the most comfortable and easy-going, and that the food was superb.

There were not many rooms. Some were in the form of apartments, large enough for a family and a servant, who might stay for weeks. Some were merely simple single rooms, mostly used by officers, businessmen and other transitory people, who would often leave a few belongings in the hotel's care for use whenever they might happen to be passing by again. A year or more might elapse between these visitations, but the guest would always find his needs anticipated, his preferences remembered, his aversions avoided. Once Louisa became attached to her guests — individuals or families — she made certain that they lacked nothing they desired. If she took a dislike to anyone, though, that person would assuredly never find a vacancy at the Bentinck again.

She herself made no effort to change. There was no attempt to learn to speak 'proper', or acquire any of the many graces she lacked. She could afford to dress well, and did, and to be generous with champagne, which she was, and to be magnanimous towards any of her favourites who, through brief or prolonged financial setback, could not manage to pay their bills. But, basically, she was what she was, and people had to accept her as it: abrasive, impulsive, outspoken, rough-tongued — she would not hesitate to address a titled person in the vernacular she used amongst the stallholders at Covent Garden. She had her own set of values, and they were mostly the right ones. Experience and shrewd observation had taught this sharp-witted, determined and ever-ambitious young woman, still in her twenties, that the quality of people could be judged just as accurately as that of any vegetable or cut of meat, once you knew the points to watch out for.

Louisa was not what all men would call beautiful, but she possessed a charisma which made her attractive to many. A few who made approaches to her, not knowing her, got sharply taken aback as soon as she opened her mouth. Her speech had nothing at all in common with her looks or the expense of her dresses. The few who, aware of this, still fancied their chances with her, were swiftly disabused. She didn't take offence, except on one or two occasions. More likely, she would turn the proposition into an excuse for some rather coarse ribbing, and would then assuage her suitor's embarrassment with the best champagne.

In a way, then, she was an eccentric: a woman of a kind unique to most who met her. A few were repelled by her and passed her hastily by. Many more were amused and attracted, though, and Louisa's personality became to them the chief magnetic force of the Bentinck. They admired her for her lack of assumed airs and graces, revelled in her bouts of outrageousness, and, in time of distress or perplexity, knew that her earthy sympathy and wisdom would be unstintingly at their disposal.

It seemed only natural — though it had all been quite coincidental — that she should have surrounded herself with a staff of semi-eccentrics. Not that this could be said of Mary Philips, her pretty young Welsh second-in-command, who had fled to her from an oppressive household where they had both been in service; and those out of sight in the kitchen regions were as healthily normal a lot as could have been collected anywhere in London. But it was those male employees with whom guests had daily personal dealings who seemed to bear something of Louisa's brand-mark.

There was Merriman, the deaf and incredibly ancient waiter, who had fought in the Crimea and probably lost there whatever merriment might ever have been in him to match his name. All day and evening he would be on the go, carrying meals, champagne, letters, newspapers, up and down the stairs, grumbling, uttering baleful prophecies, answering questions with almost monosyllabic unhelpfulness. He should have been in retirement years ago, but Louisa knew he had nowhere else to go, no one to look after him, no wish to do anything but go on working at the Bentinck, the only home he had ever known, until he should die there. She had not the kind of heart which would permit her to send him away and take on someone young, efficient and nimble. So he went on trudging the stairs on whose carpets his feet had inflicted so much wear over the years, and Louisa winked at people behind his back and said, knowing that he couldn't hear her, that he was a daft old codger who ought to be out to grass.

Starr, the porter, was a man in his early middle age, with a military bearing. He had virtually engaged himself one day, at a time when Louisa had been too inexperienced to know how to conduct an interview. He had given practically no information about himself, and when asked for references had replied that he was his own reference. He had interrogated her about the rest of the staff and the conditions of work, and then — and this was Starr's chief trait of eccentricity — consulted his dog as to whether or not they should accept the post. The animal had evidently signified in the affirmative, for Starr had been a familiar figure at the Bentinck's hall desk ever since. His nondescript little dog, Fred, was always at his side, available for consultation or to give his extra-sensory opinion of any entering stranger by barking, growling, or wagging his tail.

The other principal member of the male 'staff' was another soldierly type, though of the officer class. Major Smith-Barton, DSO, had been a resident at the hotel for some time when his preoccupation with the racing pages of the newspapers finally brought him down to Louisa's office to confess that he couldn't pay his large outstanding bill. Again, the maternal instinct in her which could only manifest itself through kindness to people down on their luck had caused Louisa to offer him an undefined job, which meant he could live on in his modest room in return for a range of duties. Some of his former Army and county friends, arriving to stay at the Bentinck, were astonished to have their bags carried to their rooms by Smith-Barton, offering no explanation but cheerfully passing on social gossip and asking how well the trout were rising this season.

When not actually occupied, the major communed much at the desk with Starr (and, of course, Fred) over the sporting pages. Louisa felt no resentment that he still had his little flutter with money which he might well have been using to pay her back. She found him a useful sort of social secretary, able to liaise on equal terms with some of the more upper-crust guests.

And so, for the couple of years since the new Lord Haslemere had moved back into permanent residence, the Bentinck had continued to prosper. Louisa still undertook outside cooking engagements, though she was able to be more and more selective now, and left most of the work to Mary Philips and the new cook, Mrs Cochrane, who had replaced Mrs Wellkin. But she had discontinued the factory-like process of baking scores of quail pies and other specialities every day for a leading grocer nearby, who sold them at a profit. That demanding trade had served its purpose at a time when finances had been low, squandered by Augustus Trotter. It had, in fact, almost killed Louisa through the overwork it entailed. But the breakdown she had suffered had led to Charlie Tyrrell reappearing in her life, which in turn had led to her becoming proprietress of the Bentinck. She could be thankful to Mr Mather, then, for once giving her regular pie-making business; but now she no longer needed it, so gave it up, to the dismay of Mr Mather and his customers.

So, in the summer of 1904, Louisa Trotter, *née* Leyton, was a contented young woman. She was still young, though heading for her thirties now, an age at which many women begin to look more searchingly at themselves in mirrors, and, if unattached, feel some symptoms of panic. Not so Louisa. As to her looks and age, she took such things for granted. She had gone through matrimony and maternity, and that was enough of that. Her early ambition had been to become the best cook in London. For many people's tastes, she was that now, and the proprietress, into the bargain, of one of London's most affectionately regarded hotels.

If there was anything else she wanted, she didn't know what it was. From now on she would be content to live from day to day, letting each bring its problems, its surprises, its amusements, its dramas, its rewards.

# CHAPTER TWO

Starr came from behind the hall desk to attend to a young man who had just come through the swing doors from the street and was glancing about in obvious unfamiliarity with the surroundings. The newcomer was strikingly handsome with a foreign look to him and his clothing, a grey overcoat with an astrakhan collar. But when he answered Starr's enquiry as to whether he might help him, he spoke with only the faintest trace of an accent. His English was perfect, almost to the point of over-correctness.

'Are you Starr, by any chance?'

Starr was surprised. The dog, Fred, looked interested. He had evinced no signs of like or animosity. 'Yes, sir.'

'I thought so. I am Baron Oppendorf. Lord Haslemere told me all about you. He said I am to trust you in everything except your advice on horses.'

Starr smiled with gratification and Fred wagged his tail.

'If you wouldn't mind waiting here one moment, sir, I'm sure Mrs Trotter would like to welcome you personally and show you to his lordship's rooms. She's been looking forward to you coming.'

The baron nodded and Starr went away to Louisa's parlour, returning almost at once, to say, 'Excuse me, sir, Mrs Trotter would very much like to welcome you in her room. If you'd kindly step this way.'

In Louisa's parlour the baron bent over her hand. 'My dear Mrs Trotter,' he said, 'this is indeed a pleasure.'

'It's nice to have you, Baron,' she replied warmly. Any friend of Charlie's was automatically an instant friend of hers. 'How long will you be staying?'

'Oh, a few days. Perhaps a week. I have come over especially for important conferences — with my tailor and my shirtmaker.'

Louisa laughed. This was the kind of free-and-easy talk she liked to hear. Nothing arrogant; merely nonchalant self-assurance. It was a quality Charlie himself possessed. And, like him, this man was agreeable to look at and knew his manners.

'I'll show you to Lord Haslemere's rooms,' she said. 'How is he?'

'In the very best of health. He sends you his kindest regards. Since he saved the old Marchese Fantucci from drowning when her carriage went careering into the harbour, he is the toast of Monte Carlo…'

He was startled to hear a voice, in a thick American accent, say from apparently nowhere, 'Monte Carlo? Who said Monte Carlo?'

From the depths of a wing chair a male figure struggled into sight. It was that of a thick-set, middle-aged man, who got to his feet with a little difficulty, burdened as he was with a jeroboam of champagne in one hand and a glass in the other. The vast bottle was half empty, the baron noticed — and a jeroboam holds not less than ten quarts of wine. He was not surprised that the man swayed a little.

'Don't mind him,' Louisa was saying. 'He's only a senator. Hey, Senator, meet Baron … Baron Oppitoff.'

The baron grinned and didn't trouble to correct her. Charlie Haslemere had told him plenty about Louisa's ways. The senator, after pausing to consider how to manage things, succeeded in. placing the bottle on the carpet and came forward, hand outstretched.

'Honoured to make your acquaintance, Baron,' he said. 'Deeply honoured.'

'Well?' Louisa admonished him. 'Aren't you going to offer the baron a drink?'

'Indeed, I am! Must have a drink from my very first — what's it called, Mrs Trotter, ma'am?'

'Cherrybum,' Louisa answered wickedly.

'That's right,' he said gravely. 'My first cherrybum. A real live cherrybum for a real live genuine baron.'

With difficulty, and a good deal of assistance from the others, he was enabled to dispense drinks for them all. They toasted one another and chatted convivially for a quarter of an hour, until Louisa firmly packed the senator and his jeroboam off to his room while she showed the new arrival to Lord Haslemere's suite, where he found that Starr had already placed his baggage, fetched from his cab.

Late that night, Starr yawned at the desk and looked at the time. Fred was already asleep in his little basket beside the porter's chair. The timeless Merriman came shuffling down the stairs.

'More for Number 3?' Starr anticipated.

The waiter nodded. 'Whisky, after all that champagne. The American gent appears to have hollow legs.'

'Better his head than mine in the morning,' Starr said. 'What're he and the baron doing up there?'

'Playing solo poker. And the American's using marked cards.'

Merriman moved off to the dispense. Starr prodded Fred gently with his boot. 'Come on, old son,' he said gently to the yawning terrier. 'Christen your lamp-post for the last time, and then we'll shut up shop and go to bed.'

Yawning man and yawning dog went out into the summer warmth of the street, still busy with cabs and carriages, fashionable strollers, noisy young bloods and urgent prostitutes.

Upstairs in the Bentinck, in Lord Haslemere's sitting room, the senator and the baron were concentrating seriously on their game. Empty whisky glasses were at their elbows and a half-empty soda syphon was to hand. Paul Oppendorf had quite a stack of banknotes beside him also. A smaller pile lay before the senator. Paul appeared to be having the best of things.

'Raise you ten,' he said.

The senator shot him a glance of apprehension, then frowned over his own hand for some moments before saying 'Double you.'

Paul said promptly, 'I'll see you.'

Merriman entered with a fresh bottle of whisky and more soda as the senator spread out his cards on the green baize table top. The baron peered at them. 'Oh, you have a flush. Is that right?'

'No, no, Baron. Three queens and two tens. A full house, queens high.'

'Ah, I see,' the baron said, showing his own hand. 'Then you are too good for me, I think.'

The senator leaned over to look. ''Fraid so,' he said, scooping up the stake money. 'About time, too, though. You had me worried there.'

'Beginner's luck, I suppose,' the baron said resignedly. 'Thank you, Merriman, I'm sure this is all we shall need tonight.'

The old man nodded and withdrew. He recognised perfectly well the real game that was being played. The American had been allowing his opponent to win steadily, giving him confidence to put down higher and higher stakes. Before they were through that new bottle of whisky, he knew, all that money would be on the senator's side of the table, and maybe an IOU as well.

'A few hands of bezique and a game of picquet with my old great-aunt, the princess — that's about all the cards that are allowed in my family,' the baron told his guest. 'I like this game. It's good of you to teach it to me. Oh, please help yourself, Senator.'

The American poured himself neat whisky and passed the bottle over to the other, who poured carefully for himself and added a good deal of soda. The senator, while far from being drunk despite having achieved the ambition of finishing off the jeroboam, was in rather less than full control of his tongue. He became confidential.

'I'm not a real senator, you know, Baron. That's just one of Mrs Trotter's wry little jokes. My name's Croker. Collis C Croker.'

Paul rose to his feet. He lurched as he did and clutched at the table edge to steady himself. Then he stood swaying as they shook hands. If he had not had the best part of two gallons of champagne and more than half a bottle of whisky inside him, the American might have noted that his drinking partner seemed to have become affected strangely suddenly. In truth, Paul was not affected at all. He had sensed a change in the wind of circumstance, and it seemed better to act the part while it continued to blow.

'I am … delighted to make your acquaintance, Mr Crocker … Croker,' he said thickly.

'Call me Collis, eh?'

'Collis.'

'I'm gratified, the senator said gravely. I'm just a country boy from Cedar Rapids, Iowa. Made my pile canning beef. Chicago. *CCC, the Best Beef there BE!* Expect you've heard of it.'

'Oh, but naturally. All over Europe.'

Collis C Croker beamed. 'CCC. That's me.'

'Very successful.'

'Sure. Only one thing wrong with my life, Baron.'

'What is that?'

'My wife. She's been took religious. She's took religious and she's took against drink. Nearly ruined my life. Had to invent this trip to Europe just to save my sanity.'

The baron tut-tutted and poured his friend another neat whisky. It went unnoticed that he added nothing to his own glass.

'Say, Baron, you don't mind if I ask what you do?'

'Do?'

'For a living?'

The aristocratic eyebrows were raised high with surprise. 'My dear chap, I do nothing for a living. None of my family has, that I have ever heard of. Not for several hundred years, at any rate. You see, we have always had big estates in Bohemia and Thuringia. Money and commerce are things we never mention at home.' He raised a deprecatory hand. 'Oh, of course my family must have had to amass money at some time. Everyone who is rich must have had ancestors who made fortunes in the past. Or rather, not so much made them, as won them — the gift of kings and emperors for battles fought victoriously, for fleets of ships captured laden with treasure.'

The senator was shaking his head in undisguised wonderment. The baron took a pull at his glass, contriving, however, not to let any of the whisky actually pass his lips. He continued, 'In fact, I can only think of one of my forebears who made money: my great-uncle Philip. He did literally make money.'

'Well, I guess even in the richest families, there's always one guy who…'

'No, no, no, no. I mean, he actually *made* money.'

The senator goggled, as well as his by-now impaired vision would allow. 'You mean … he had a … a mint, of his own?'

The baron contrived a grim smile. 'I think … Collis … it's a story better hidden in the mists of time. Not a very creditable chapter in my family's history. I should never have alluded to it.'

But the American was totally intrigued by now. He leaned his elbows on the baize. 'Look, Baron, I won't think no worse of you, or of your family. I've sailed pretty close to the wind once or twice myself.'

Paul returned his waveringly intense gaze for some moments. Then he shrugged, took a cigar from his case, pierced it and lit it carefully. At last he said, 'Well, towards the end of the eighteenth century it became clear to my great-uncle Philip that the foreman on one of his estates had hired a young man with a genius for invention. My great-uncle Philip, being a philanthropic sort of man, sent the boy to study in Vienna, where he quickly astonished his professors with his inventions. One of them was a machine for reproducing paper money. A sort of … magic box.'

The senator whistled. 'That's a useful kind of toy! I wish people could still make toys like that. Anyway, it probably would seem pretty crude work nowadays.'

'Oh, no. It doesn't.'

'Doesn't? You mean…'

'The machine still exists.' Paul nodded.

'Gee! Somewhere on the Continent?'

'As a matter of fact, no. It's here in London. Safe in a vault. You see, my family acquired it. It passed to me from my late father. On his deathbed he made me promise always to take it with me, wherever I might go. He himself put it into my hands.'

Moved by more than one sort of reverence, the senator said, 'What I'd give to see it. You … you couldn't…? No, of course not.'

'What?'

'Allow me the very special privilege of just seeing it — once?'

The baron appeared shocked. He shook his head. 'It is a matter of strict principle. You understand what I mean?'

'I guess so. It's just that, well, to see something so historic — unique, in fact — why, that would really cap my trip to Europe. I guess I could even face my wife again after that.'

Paul laughed. 'Collis, I like you. You're open. I trust you.'

'Thanks, Baron. May I say, on my part, I feel a bond of friendship has already been forged between us.'

His young companion seemed to reach a sudden decision. 'All right. If it would really amuse you so much, I'll bring it here the day after tomorrow.'

'To … to this very room?'

'Strictly for your eyes alone, you understand.'

'I'd be most deeply honoured, sir.'

The American's eyes looked regretfully at the pile of money at the other side of the table. If they hadn't spent so much time chatting, it would have been added to his own by now. Still, there was bound to be another encounter. Perhaps more than one. And if money was no object to this amiable young fellow…

But he merely indicated the whisky bottle. 'Mind if I take a little of this along with me? Just a settler for the night.'

'Take the bottle, my dear chap. I shan't be requiring any more.'

Later next morning, 'Senator' Collis C Croker went eagerly to Lord Haslemere's suite, where his new friend, the baron, welcomed him affably. To the senator's regret, the baron had not been visible all the previous day and evening. At least one chance to win back his poker losses had passed by, but he had further, greater expectations.

'You've got the machine?' he half-whispered, although they were behind the closed door now. Paul nodded.

The senator felt relief. He had half expected that, in more sober mood, the baron would have reversed his decision. However, Paul's expression was serious as he said, 'I must ask you to give me your word that everything you see or hear in this room in the next few minutes will go no further than these walls?

'Surely I will, sir.'

The baron went to unlock a lacquered chinoiserie cupboard. From one of its many compartments he drew out the magic box. It was quite small and plain, of polished wood, with no obvious gadgetry revealed, apart from some small brass dials and a plunger. There were three little drawers and a keyhole. The senator did not presume to touch it, but contented himself with peering keenly at it.

'Beautiful piece of work,' he said.

'Isn't it? And here is one of the first notes the boy made with it.'

The baron was holding out a beautifully designed old Austrian banknote. The senator took it and examined it closely.

It was flawlessly printed. He handed it back. 'How many of these boxes did that young fellow make?'

'Only this one. Shortly after the boy made it he … he met with a fatal accident — arranged, some say, by my great-great-uncle. You see, philanthropist though he was, he was also a practical man, who believed that for the good of mankind, there are some people who are better dead than alive. If many of these boxes had been produced and had fallen into unscrupulous hands … well, you can imagine the fiscal chaos which might have ensued — throughout the whole world, even.'

'I guess your uncle had his head screwed on the right way,' the senator nodded.

'Even now,' the baron continued, 'the responsibility of its custodianship is a constant worry to me. Wherever I go — and I am a widely travelled man — it must go, too. It only requires me to be careless once and leave a lock unsecured, or suffer some little forgetfulness, and…' He shrugged meaningfully. 'I suppose it should be kept in some bank vault, but what is the point of that? If it is never to see the light of day again, it might just as well be destroyed. In fact, I have considered —'

'No, no!' the American begged hastily, obviously alarmed. 'Not that!'

Paul shrugged again.

After a few more moments' contemplation of the intriguing object, the senator said, 'Why not donate it to some scientific museum? So that all the world could admire it, without any danger of its being put to the wrong use?'

He waited for the baron to consider this. The answer at length was. 'No, no. It was entrusted to me, and I feel it my duty to honour that trust, however much trouble it costs me.'

'Well, I respect you for that, Baron. In any case, maybe it wouldn't even work any more, so there's no real risk.'

'Oh, but it does. It's in perfect working order. Naturally, I have only used it a very few times, simply to amuse my friends.'

The senator swallowed. 'I suppose … you wouldn't count me enough of a friend to … to give me the great privilege of a demonstration?'

Paul studied him for some moments, not condescendingly, but as if needing to struggle hard with his own judgment. At last he smiled and said, 'Why not?

The senator just restrained himself from rubbing his hands with glee. In his most serious tone he said, 'I'm deeply honoured, Baron. Both to be counted so close a friend, and…' Emotion almost overcame him. He managed to add, 'I swear solemnly not to reveal this to a living soul.'

Paul was opening one of the little drawers in the machine and taking out some blank slips of paper of various sizes. 'Might I trouble you,' he asked, 'for the loan of a note? Any denomination. Preferably little used.'

Collis C Croker's wallet was out swiftly and a freshly minted ten-pound note handed over. The baron held it against two or three of the slips of blank paper until he found one which exactly matched its size. Then he handed the note back, saying, 'Please be so good as to note the serial number of your note. I assure you no harm will come to your money.'

From opposite sides of the machine he pulled out two more drawers. Into one he placed the banknote; into the other went the blank. He closed the drawers. Then he took out his key chain, selected a small key, inserted it in the keyhole of the machine and began to wind carefully.

'Of course, the secret of how it works died with its inventor. The mechanism is activated by clockwork. The process takes twelve hours precisely. So —' he carried the machine carefully back to its cupboard — 'we will leave it in peace, and I hope you will pay me another visit this evening?'

'Surely! I don't know how I'll stick the waiting.'

'Well, we could pass the first half an hour or so of it by having a drink, if it isn't too early for you?'

But the senator, for whom no time was too early for a drink, for once declined. 'If you'll pardon me, Baron. I have to be off to a luncheon engagement. Till this evening, though.'

Paul locked the door and returned to the cupboard in which his magic box lay. He took it out, slid out one of the drawers, and extracted the ten-pound note. He put the machine away again and carried the note to his desk top. From a drawer of the desk he took out a leather case of a size and shape which might have suited it for carrying surgical instruments. It did, in fact, contain instruments, surgical in appearance but not intended for that purpose. It also held a pair of thin gloves and a jeweller's eyeglass.

Paul took out his own wallet and examined all the ten-pound notes it contained. Most of them he had won from the American in their poker game. He had noted then that they were a freshly minted batch, obviously just withdrawn from a bank. As he had expected, their numbers belonged to the same series. It did not take him long to find one whose number differed by only one digit from that which Croker had lent him.

Also from his instrument case, Paul extracted a piece of ground glass, clipped into its lid. He put this on his desk in front of him and on it, side by side, the two banknotes. Then he donned the gloves, screwed the eyeglass into his right eye, selected one of the instruments — which he dipped into one of several phials of different coloured liquids — and, with infinite care and a rock-steady hand, proceeded to alter that one digit in the second note's serial number to correspond with its fellow on the other. When he had finished, no one but an expert could have detected the forgery.

# CHAPTER THREE

Exactly twelve hours after he had left Baron Oppendorf's suite, Collis C Croker returned to it. He found himself almost trembling with an anticipation which had been mounting all day, and which he had endeavoured to calm with the aid of generous doses of spirituous liquors.

Paul received him graciously. He locked the door and fetched the box from its cupboard and placed it on his desk. 'Now,' he said, 'this part is rather complicated, so please do not speak for a few moments. I have to concentrate to get it precisely right.'

The senator all but held his breath as he watched the baron, frowning with concentration, adjust the brass dials in turn. Finally he pressed home the plunger and straightened up. A faint whirring sound was heard.

'Now we wait ten seconds,' he said, counting them mentally. A sharp click from the box almost made the senator jump. Paul quickly drew out the side drawers. A ten-pound note lay in each.

'Please do not touch them,' he instructed. 'They are still wet. But look closely, and see if they are not identical.'

The American obeyed. He took out his pocket book and checked the serial number of his original note. Both of these now revealed to him bore it. To his eyes, they were identical in every way.

'Well, I'll be doggoned!' he exclaimed. 'Which is the false one?'

'Neither is false,' Paul told him. 'One is an exact copy of the other, that is all. They are equally valid as legal tender.' He laughed. 'Unless anyone were indiscreet enough to tender them both at once, of course. Even so, not even an expert could identify the copy from the original.' He peered closer at the notes. 'They are quite dry now,' he said. He picked one out and handed it to the senator. 'There you are — your note returned — or is it?'

They laughed heartily together.

Paul said, 'I think I had better retain the other. The risk of your accidentally spending two identical notes simultaneously is too great to run. No, on second thoughts, take the other, too. Having seen the miracle performed, I think you are entitled to put the result to the test. Go to two separate banks. At each of them, show a cashier one — only one — of the notes, saying you have heard rumours that there are forgeries about and you wish to be sure that your note is genuine. I guarantee that in each case the answer will be that it is.'

The senator demurred. 'No, no, Baron. I can see with my own eyes. Anyway, why should I doubt your word?'

'Thank you. All the same, I should like you to do as I suggest. I promise you it will bring you even greater satisfaction.'

'Well, I guess that's true. I'll go straight away in the morning.' He placed the notes in separate compartments of his wallet. 'Say, how about that return match of poker meanwhile? So long as I don't let you win either of these notes off me.'

Paul shook his head regretfully. 'I'm sorry, Collis, but I really must decline. I have a long and complicated business letter to write which will take me half the night. Tomorrow evening, though?'

'Well, sure. Something else to look forward to.'

Paul bowed acknowledgment, unlocked the door and let him out. As he did so, Merriman approached him, carrying a tray of sandwiches and coffee. Paul stood aside to let him in.

Merriman's gaze fell on the mysterious box on the desk. Paul saw it, but noticed that the rheumy old eyes flickered away again without showing curiosity or interest.

'Porridge and devilled kidneys for breakfast as usual, sir?' the waiter asked.

'Thank you. Is that all, Merriman?'

'Yes, sir. Good night, sir.'

Starr looked down at his dog behind the hall desk the next morning as a beaming Senator Croker bustled past, making for the stairs.

'Senator's in a hurry today, Fred,' he observed.

The dog nodded. He, too, had noticed the American hurry out of the hotel a few minutes before bank opening time.

Paul was reading a letter and smoking a cheroot over the remains of his habitually late breakfast. He wore his dressing gown over his tieless shirt and trousers. When he heard the excited knock at the passage door he smiled and tore up the letter, putting the fragments on to one of his plates. 'Come in,' he called. As he had anticipated, his visitor was Collis C Croker.

'It's a goddamn miracle, Baron!' that gentleman blurted out as he bustled into the room. He closed the door, then hurried over to the table, tugging out his wallet and saying, 'I went to the Bank of America and the First National Bank of Chicago. Both chief cashiers said the notes are genuine.'

He held them out. Paul said, 'Of course.' He reached forward, took one of them from the senator's hand and tore it into small fragments, which he scattered amongst the pieces of letter on the plate.

'Hey!' the American cried. 'That's a waste!'

'My dear Collis, I told you how dangerous it would be to risk having two identical notes in circulation. It could set off a needless alarm about widespread forgeries which might even do harm to the national currency. In any case, what are ten pounds to you or me —' He broke off abruptly, then resumed, 'Although —'

'What is it, Baron?'

'Oh, it merely struck me suddenly that the richest people in the world can sometimes be really the poorest — in terms of ready money.'

The senator regarded him with new interest. 'You aren't short of cash yourself, Baron?'

'Certainly not. That is to say … well, perhaps unwisely, I have tied up so much capital in investments which will bear great fruit in the medium term that, at this moment, I am a relatively poor man in the everyday sense.'

The senator grinned. 'Well, you're gonna be poorer after we get to that poker game, I promise you.' Then, suddenly serious, he added, 'If you ever do need money — cash — I'll buy that box off of you, at a really handsome price.'

Paul shook his head firmly. 'Oh, no. No question of that. I told you, it's a question of family honour.'

'Family honour's a damn tough thing for a man like me to understand, Baron. Cash on the nail isn't.'

Paul stood up. 'No, I'm sorry, Collis. Now, if you'll excuse me, I have to finish dressing. I have an appointment with my bootmaker.'

'And with me tonight.' The American grinned again. 'Say ten? And this time the whisky's on me.'

An hour after this, Louisa sat in her parlour contemplating a ten-pound note. Or rather, the ruins of one. It was pieced together on the blotter on her desk. Merriman stood beside her chair.

'Talk about throwing money away!' she exclaimed. 'Merriman, for a man that looks like a desiccated old bat, you've got remarkably sharp eyes.'

'It was noticing all that paper on the plate when I cleared up,' he replied modestly. 'If you take my meaning, ma'am, eyes are there to be used.' He paused for breath and then, uncharacteristically, prolonged his speech. 'There is another aspect of the gentleman in Number 3, if you could spare five minutes, ma'am.'

Louisa eyed him critically. 'Proper old busybody you're getting in your dotage, aren't you? All right. Let's have it.'

In one of the longest speeches he had achieved in years, Merriman described how, in serving the gentleman his coffee and sandwiches the evening before, he had chanced to observe on the gentleman's desk a box. He described it: polished wood, little drawers, brass dials, plunger thing in the top. He went on to recall how, many, many years before, while working as a steward in the first-class dining saloon of a liner, he had seen just such an object in the cabin of a passenger, a foreign gentleman he remembered distinctly, to whom he had been serving champagne.

'And when we reached the River Plate in South America, ma'am, the police came on board and arrested the foreign gentleman and his box. And then they came back and examined every single piece of paper money on the ship, and took some of it away. And when we came that way again, next time round, we was told the man had been given years in jail for forgery and all something to do with that box of his.'

'Sherlock Holmes and all,' Louisa mocked him.

'Thank you, ma'am,' Merriman said. 'So, don't you think there might be something funny about the gentleman in Number 3, too? I mean, perhaps you ought to warn him off, ma'am, or we'll have the police coming here.'

'Warn him off?' Louisa flared ungratefully at him. 'Look, Merriman, you're the waiter here, not the bloody manager. What people do or don't do in my hotel is their business — and mine.'

All the same, she sent a telegram to Charlie Haslemere in Monte Carlo concerning the gentleman in Number 3.


The return poker game duly took place. To the senator's consternation, though, the baron produced an expensive new pack of cards. He said he had seen them while shopping that day and couldn't resist buying them. Regretfully, the senator had to return his own carefully marked pack to his pocket. He cursed himself for not having turned the tables on his opponent earlier in that first encounter: he had let him go on winning too long.

The beginner's luck seemed to be persisting, too. The baron won the first three hands, displaying seemingly ingenuous delight each time. In the fourth, the stakes began to mount high as neither player cracked. Just as the senator was beginning to feel genuinely worried, Paul asked innocently, 'May I double again?'

'Well, sure — if you really want to.'

'I think so.' Paul doubled the stake.

It was too much for the senator's nerve. 'See you,' he sighed.

Paul laid out his hand. To his opponent's great relief it was no match for his. Only a novice would have run the stakes so high on the strength of it.

Wistfully, Paul pushed all the money across the table. 'The tide really seems to have turned,' he said. 'Another loss or two like that, and I shall scarcely be able to pay my bill here. Collis, would it be too ungentlemanly of me to withdraw from the game?'

The American poured whisky for them both and uncased a fresh cigar. He leaned back expansively. 'Men have been shot for less where I was raised,' he grinned. 'But it ain't in the nature of Collis C Croker to take advantage of a greenhorn, at poker or anything else. Sure we'll stop. In any case, Baron, there's something more serious than cards I'd like to talk about with you.'

Paul lit his own cigar and waited.

The senator spoke carefully and seriously. 'All the day, I haven't been able to put that box of yours out of my mind. That box is of great historic interest — too great for it to be permanently hidden away from view. Ever since I set foot in Europe I've been greatly impressed at the sense of history and tradition all around me, and I've been thinking today what a shame it would be if so many of those great treasures of your heritage just weren't out there for ordinary folk like me to come along and marvel at. Now, I guess we all would like to leave behind us on this earth a little something to be remembered by. CCC canned beef will live on, of course, but it seems to me there should be something more than that. So I've decided to build a museum. The Collis C Croker Museum of Science, bang in the middle of one of the greatest cities in the world, Chicago.'

'That is a very noble idea,' Paul said.

The American nodded. 'People are going to come from all over the civilised world to see that museum. And shall I tell you what one of the chief attractions will be? It will be the Oppendorf Room, preserving the name of your noble and illustrious family for ever more. And bang in the centre of that display, for all the world to marvel at, will be that magic little box of yours. Now, Baron, what would you say to twenty thousand dollars — in cash?'

He waited breathlessly as the nobleman pondered, obviously deeply tempted.

'It's a generous offer — thirty thousand dollars,' Paul said at length.

The senator took the hint. 'Done, then?'

Paul sighed. 'Very well.'

They shook hands warmly and toasted one another in whisky.

Late the following evening the senator was back in Paul's room yet again. This time he brought with him a case containing thirty thousand dollars in notes. He insisted on counting the whole lot out as he piled the mound of paper on the desk. In return, Paul handed over the box.

'I hope I'm doing the right thing,' he said hesitantly.

'Sure you are, Baron. The world will thank you. Now, have you the instructions, please?'

Paul replied, 'I've written them out, as you requested. But it has occurred to me since that since you will not actually be using the box, and as a safeguard, perhaps it might be better not —'

The senator interrupted quickly, 'It will be more interesting, historically and scientifically, to have them framed beside the exhibit itself. You have my word that no other person will get access to the box.'

Paul nodded and handed over an envelope. He detached the key from his chain as well.

'Thanks, Baron. When I have the museum built, I'll have you come over and open it, if you will.'

Paul gave his little bow. 'I shall look forward to that great day. You can always find me via the Ritz in Paris.'

They shook hands again and parted company, each man more than satisfied with his side of the deal. A short while afterwards Paul went down to Louisa's parlour. She was just in time to push under her blotter a long telegram she had received from Monte Carlo.

'Hello, Baron,' she greeted him cheerfully. 'Hope you're enjoying your stay in London?'

'I have done, Mrs Trotter. Very much. Unfortunately, it must now come to an end. I should be grateful for my bill the first thing in the morning, please.'

Louisa chuckled. 'I'm glad of that.'

He raised his eyebrows.

'Save me having to throw you out, that's why.'

He stared uncomprehendingly for some moments, then gave her his most winning smile. 'You British. I shall never understand you.'

'No, you wouldn't,' Louisa said, searching for a piece of paper. 'Here's your bill. All ready.'

He looked at her quizzically, then at the bill. 'Ninety-two guineas! But that is far too much.'

'No, it ain't. Not considering.'

'Considering what, madam?'

'That you're not a baron, no more than I am.' She fished out the telegram from Charlie. '"Baron Oppendorf", alias "Count Ginsky", alias "Prince Zhanovsky" … highly titled, your family. You see, I wired to your friend and mine, Charlie

Haslemere, to make some enquiries. He says he's discovered you're nothing but a common little crook, wanted by the French police for crimes too numerous to recount. He advises me to inform Scotland Yard immediately.'

Though shaken, Paul could reply, 'Which, being a sensible woman and mindful of the reputation of your hotel, you have not done?'

'No.'

'And won't do?'

'That depends. I don't promise nothing. Who are you, "Baron"? Let's have it.'

He smiled and shrugged. 'A soldier of fortune, fighting the good fight in the battle of life. My father kept a livery stable at Hounslow. I grew up to prefer women and money to horses. So, much to my father's disdain and anger, I went into service.'

Louisa smiled. 'We've something in common, then.'

'I was taken to Amsterdam by a diplomat as his valet and soon found how easily greedy men are parted from their money. Our dear old "senator", for instance.'

'So, you've sold him your rotten old box,' Louisa laughed. 'How much? Twenty — thirty thousand dollars? Never mind shrugging your shoulders all innocent like that. Here,' she half-whispered, 'what was in the box really? I won't tell no one.'

Paul relaxed at last. 'We are two of a kind, aren't we?'

'No. Not quite. We both give 'em what they want, and we make 'em pay for it. But I do it straight, and you cheat 'em. It's a bit different, you know.'

'I suppose so. Well, a little joiner in Brussels knocks them up for me quite cheaply. A failed craftsman, I often think, when I look at the quality of his work. A beautiful box, some simple clockwork, a couple of rollers and some drawers. The skill is mine.'

'Profitable sideline, though.'

'Exactly,' Paul admitted. 'I sold five last year. Men who are really greedy for money will buy anything, and when our friend the "senator" tried to cheat me at poker — me, of all people! — using marked cards, I thought he needed teaching a lesson.'

Louisa grinned and reached down beside her desk. A champagne bottle lay there in a bucket of ice. 'Open it for us, will you, ducks?' she asked. He obeyed as she produced two gleaming glasses from a small cupboard beside her. 'Where are you off to this time?' she asked, as the cork came out and the chilled wine was poured.

'Lisbon. From there, who knows? The world is my oyster — or most of it is.'

'Have you thought,' she asked, as they silently toasted one another, 'that the first thing he'll do, now he's got your machine, is try it out? And when it doesn't work, he'll be round to your room like a bat out of hell.'

Paul sipped and smiled. 'The process takes twelve hours,' he said. 'Anything less than that would be bound to be a failure. And within twelve hours, with the benefit of an early call and an admirable early breakfast from you, madam, I shall no longer be on the premises to try to explain how he must have made some mistake in the rather complicated operation.'

'Cheeky devil!' Louisa said. 'Here, let's have that bill back a minute.'

He handed it over. She picked up a pen and added a final nought to the total before handing the bill back.

'Nine hundred and twenty guineas!' he exclaimed. 'This … this is sheer blackmail.'

'Yes, dear,' Louisa smiled. 'Though what a rude word to use to a lady. If it's more convenient, I'll take it in dollars.'

Paul regarded her for a long moment. She raised the champagne bottle towards his glass. After the briefest hesitation he advanced the glass and allowed her to pour for him. He raised the glass in salute, sipped, then got out his wallet and counted four thousand dollars from his hoard. When he had placed them before her he took her hand and kissed it.

'Goodbye, Mrs Trotter,' he said. 'It has been a pleasure to know you.'

'Goodbye, "Baron",' Louisa returned. 'I hope I never set eyes on you again.'

# CHAPTER FOUR

Louisa was proud of her king, although she rarely saw him nowadays, having reduced her outside catering even more, and also because he was tending to spend an increasing amount of time abroad. After the long, frustrating years of waiting for the throne, he had confounded his detractors and delighted his friends by demonstrating the natural talent for sovereignty which the former had refused to believe existed and the latter had been certain had been latent under the sporty, pleasure-seeking exterior of a man who had nothing to do but be sporty and pleasure-seeking.

In particular, he had carried his country to new popularity on the Continent, where his reclusive late mother's influence had been little felt. Treaties with Germany, Italy, Spain, Portugal and France had been concluded largely through his efforts, and the establishment of the *entente cordiale* with Britain's arch-rival, France, had been a personal triumph. 'Edward the Peacemaker', he was known as now, and Louisa Trotter recalled with pride that his slippers and dressing gown had once reposed in the wardrobe of her own bedroom.

She took little interest in politics, though. If there had been any such a thing as a woman's right to vote at this time, she would probably not have troubled to exercise it. If she had, she would instinctively have put herself down a Tory. Most of the aristocracy with whom she had contact were Tories. As a self-made woman, so to speak, the last thing she would have wished to see would be the Labour Party gaining power.

The Liberals left her indifferent. She had a vague notion that they were a party of nonconformists and teetotallers; worthy, well-meaning, but dull and ineffectual. She discovered otherwise one October evening in 1905 when she was invited to join a party in the suite of one of her semi-permanent residents, George Dugdale, a Liberal Member of Parliament.

'What's the rumpus?' Starr asked Merriman, seeing the latter making his way towards the stairs with a tray heavily laden with champagne bottles. Starr had just brought Fred in from his evening sniff round his territory. The babble of voices and laughter from upstairs was considerable.

'Them Liberals,' Merriman answered. 'Knocking back this stuff like water. Barely time to chill it.'

'All over winning a little by-election in Yorkshire?'

'Seems they reckon there's bigger things to come. Anyway, Mrs Trotter's just gone up. She'd account for half the noise.'

'Wouldn't put her down a Liberal, would you, Fred?'

The dog appeared to have no opinion.

Merriman, going on his way, said, 'Political impartiality, Mr Starr. That's what you need in this trade. Lose out on tips, otherwise.'

As he went up the stairs the hotel's front door opened and a young woman came through. She was in her late thirties, attractive and quietly dressed. Fred came out to sniff at the hem of her skirt and then returned to his basket, clearly approving.

'Good evening,' she addressed Starr. 'I'm supposed to be meeting Sir James Rosslyn here. My name is Mrs Strickland.'

'Yes, madam. You'd be the lady he's lending his rooms to for a few weeks.'

A cabbie had brought her luggage into the hall. Starr paid him off for her.

'Sir James is up in Mr Dugdale's suite just now,' he said. 'They're celebrating their by-election. I expect you can hear.'

Diana Strickland smiled.

Starr asked, 'Would you like me to fetch him, madam, or shall I show you to his rooms? They're all ready for you.'

'Let's go up, shall we?' she suggested. He picked up the baggage and led the way.

In George Dugdale's suite, the air was thick with cigar and cigarette smoke. Merriman was striving mightily to keep the glasses of the celebrating men topped up. Louisa, the only woman present, was tossing back champagne as fast as any of them. She had commandeered a bottle for herself and recharged her glass after every sip. She was already slightly flown.

She was talking to Sir James Rosslyn, a fastidious, rather puritanical old gentleman, and their host, George Dugdale. Dugdale was a complete contrast to his senior. He was only just fifty, a lawyer by profession and a comparative newcomer to the Liberal Party. His aggressive self-confidence, happily complemented by great energy and a winning charm, had got him elected to the House of Commons the previous year in a constituency which had been thought to be a Tory stronghold. His success had been one of the many at about this time which were now pointing to a close-run thing at the General Election which must soon be forthcoming.

'What I should like to know,' he was asking Louisa flippantly, 'is whether you're for us or against us?'

She laughed. 'It's your wine I'm drinking, Mr Duggy, so I'd better be for you. Mind you, I prefer Tories. They're gentlemen.'

'Wicked snob!' Dugdale accused her with a laugh. Sir James Rosslyn told her seriously, 'You'll see a Liberal government before Christmas, Mrs Trotter. We're expecting Balfour to resign within weeks.'

'You goin' to be Prime Minister, then?' she said to Dugdale.

It was Rosslyn who answered, 'Sir Henry Campbell Bannerman seems the likeliest choice.'

Starr had edged his way through the throng. 'Excuse me, Sir James,' he intervened. 'Mrs Strickland has arrived. I've shown her into your rooms.'

'Ah, thank you, Starr. I must go and settle her in. Excuse me, Mrs Trotter.'

'Bring her along here,' Louisa called to him as he moved away, ignoring the fact that it was not her party. 'I always like to welcome my guests with a glass of wine.' She winked at George Dugdale. 'And if somebody else is paying for it, so much the better.'

Merriman was passing. She reached out and took another full bottle from his hand, giving him her empty one in return. She poured for Dugdale and herself.

'Mrs Trotter,' he said, 'now you can explain the mystery of this lady Rosslyn has been fidgeting about all evening. Don't tell me the old fox has got himself a mistress.'

'What, Sir Rosy? Not likely, is it? Family friend, he said.'

'Hmm! From the front row of which chorus, I wonder?'

At that moment Sir James Rosslyn was welcoming Diana Strickland in the most decorous fashion.

'Dear James, this is perfect,' she said. 'But I feel so dreadful about turning you out of your own rooms.'

'Not at all, my dear. I'm round the corner in Albemarle Street, with my brother. So I'm on hand if you need me, though I shall be away, moving around the country a good deal. You've heard of our success at Barkston Ash today? We're on the verge of great things at last.'

'Yes, I heard. I'm so glad. Harry sends his best regards.'

'Thank you. How is he, Diana?'

'Oh, much the same. He's talking more clearly now and he can move his right arm a little. The doctors are quite hopeful.'

'Good. Now, I'm bidden by our redoubtable proprietress, Mrs Trotter, to take you over to George Dugdale's suite, where we're having a little celebration. Do you feel up to it?'

'Why not? With pleasure.'

He led her off in the direction of the noise. 'You'll find the staff here friendly, if a trifle eccentric. Don't, ah, be perturbed by Mrs Trotter. She's what is generally termed a "character", but she's first class beneath it.'

The noise and smoke hit Diana like a blast of hot wind when Sir James opened Dugdale's door. Louisa greeted her true to form.

'How d'you do? Sir Rosy, fetch her a glass. You another of these cocky Liberals, Mrs Strickland?'

'I'm not political at all,' Diana replied with equanimity. 'Just an old family friend of James, who's kindly offered to lend me his rooms for a few weeks.'

'Brought a maid, have you?'

'Oh, no.'

'Well, I'll send Mary up directly to do your unpacking. Nice kid. Welsh. Ah, thanks, Sir Rosy. Now, dear, get this down your throat and meet my friend Mr Duggy, who'll be Prime Minister in about fifty years. It's his party.'

Diana turned to George Dugdale and raised her glass to him before drinking. 'Then it's you I must thank for this,' she smiled. He was regarding her with keen interest.

'I'm so pleased to meet you, Mrs Strickland. Welcome to this gathering of distinguished and inebriate Liberals. May I ask what brings you to this notorious establishment?'

'I've come to work. I'm an artist.'

'Oh!' Louisa said. 'We had Walter Sickert here in the summer, in Number 8.'

'Heavens, I'm nowhere near that standard, Mrs Trotter. I do things for children's magazines. And Christmas cards and Valentines.'

'Do you sell?'

'Not as much as I'd like. But I'm beginning, and I'm ambitious.'

'Fascinating,' George Dugdale said. 'Does your husband encourage you?'

'He's … quite amused.'

'Only amused. Is that enough?'

'Yes, for me it is.'

Louisa could sense the probing nature of Dugdale's questioning. She rebuked him. 'Of course it's enough. How many husbands would let their wives come to London alone and get on with what they want to do, without interference?'

'Yes, indeed,' he had to concede. 'Would you allow me to see your work sometime, Mrs Strickland?'

'Now, George,' Rosslyn broke in, 'she's come here to work in peace and quiet…'

'Good lord, I won't make a nuisance of myself. Just a glance, and I shall be satisfied.'

Sir James Rosslyn and Louisa exchanged looks. They knew George Dugdale.

Next morning, Diana, comfortably settled into the Bentinck, went out to buy some painting materials. On her way back she was accosted in the hall by Major Smith-Barton, on his way to Louisa's sanctum.

'Diana Strickland?' he enquired. 'Yes, it is. Smith-Barton. I stayed a weekend in your house some time ago.'

'Oh yes, of course. How do you do? Are you staying here?'

The major produced his ready and literally true answer to this potentially embarrassing enquiry, frequently made. 'Yes. Treat it as my London home. Sorry to hear about Harry's misfortunes. How's he getting along?'

'Oh … his illness, you mean? He's doing quite well, thank you.'

After a few more words she went away to her room. The major entered Louisa's presence with a puzzled look on his face.

'Extraordinary,' he said. 'What's Diana Strickland doing here?'

'Oh, you know her, do you, Major?'

'Yes. Charming woman. Walked out on old Harry at last, has she?'

'What?'

'Always on the cards. Don't know what she ever saw in him. Pleasant enough chap to go shooting with. Convivial. But don't ever lend him money. Not that I ever did, of course. Creditors chasing him all over Lincolnshire. They say his stroke was a stroke of luck. Kept the hounds at bay for a while.'

'So that's the way the wind blows? I don't like ladies who've left their husbands. They're trouble.' Louisa was apt not to remember that she was one herself.

'Don't take my word for it,' the major corrected her hastily. 'Just wouldn't entirely surprise me. Oh, talking of money, Mrs Trotter, I had a bit come through this morning. Thought it only right you should have it, after all your kindness. Help put the record straight a bit.' He handed her an envelope. 'Only sorry it can't be more.'

Louisa smiled up at him. 'It's the thought that counts, Major.'

A few mornings later, Mary, clearing Mrs Strickland's breakfast things from her sitting room, stared with admiration at the watercolour painting Diana was engaged upon at an easel near the window. It was of an extremely prissy-looking cat, in a bonnet and dress, admonishing two naughty kittens in children's frocks.

'Ooh, that's lovely, ma'am!' the Welsh maid declared. 'Pussy with her bonnet on. My Uncle Bryn was an artist.'

'Really?' Diana was absorbed, working very fast.

'Thought of quite highly in the village, he was. He did one of me once. My mam's still got it hanging in her bedroom.' She sensed that Mrs Strickland didn't wish to be disturbed. 'Well, if there's nothing else…'

'No, thank you, Mary.'

The maid was just leaving with the tray when she encountered Mr George Dugdale in the doorway. He gave her an attractive smile.

'Morning, Mary. Is Mrs Strickland in?' He could see that she was.

'Yes, sir. Only she's…'

He walked past her, leaving the door open. 'Am I interrupting?' he asked Diana, who looked round at him. 'Just say so.'

'Not at all, Mr Dugdale.' He closed the door. Diana went on, 'Forgive me if I don't stop. I have to do my pieces at one go, or I lose myself. It's rather like painting real animals that just happen to have posed for a moment and might run off before I've got them on paper.'

'I quite understand.' He came over to look at the painting. 'Is the cat our heroine?'

'Yes. Frightful creature, always lecturing everyone on how to behave. Here she's telling the kittens they mustn't chase little birds because they're all God's creatures.'

'Hm!'

'Yes. Quite.'

'What would you rather be doing?'

'I've got a book in mind about the animals I remember from when I was a little girl in Canada. I was born there. Beavers, wolves, grizzly bears... My father used to tell me beautiful stories about them.'

'Really? Have you made any drawings of those animals?'

'Yes. Over there, in that folder. Please do have a look, if you like. They're only sketches, but I'm looking forward to working them up and writing the stories, if I can find a publisher who'd be interested.'

Dugdale picked up one of the many folders lying about and sat in a chair with it spread open across his knees. He went slowly through the loose leaves. When he had finished he said, 'These are very good. Have you shown them to any publishers yet?'

'No. I think I'd have to complete a few first, and I haven't had time yet.'

He shook his head. 'I don't think so. I have a good friend who publishes illustrated books for children. Alfred Hurst. I'm sure he'd be interested to see them just as they are and talk to you about the whole idea.'

Diana had finished her picture and cleaned her brushes. She came over to him.

He said, 'This sorrowful old bear reminds me of a certain Tory politician.'

She laughed. 'To tell you the truth, I always try to give them human features. I base them on people I know.'

'So I was right. Enchanting! Now, what time do you stop for luncheon?'

'Oh, I don't. I haven't time.'

'You must today. I'm taking you to the Savoy.'

'But…'

'James Rosslyn isn't here to look after you, so I shall. I'll call back at a quarter to one, shall I?'

Diana looked at the clock. There was ample time to get one more painting done before then. 'Very well,' she capitulated. 'That would be very nice.'

At three o'clock they had finished the meal at a discreetly positioned table for two in the Savoy Grill. They had eaten early pheasant with a superb Nuits St Georges. Now they were drinking liqueurs and George Dugdale had lit a Havana cigar.

'I found the law too easy — a game, really,' he was explaining. 'Politics is just another game, of course, but rather more fun. There was a by-election at Rye a year ago and I romped home for the Liberals, to all the local Tories' surprise. Now I'm what is called a marked man with an interesting future. I have an enormous belief in myself, as you may have guessed.'

Diana smiled. She had certainly found him self-assured during their luncheon chat, but his charm overrode any sense of arrogance. 'My husband stood as a Tory once,' she said. 'But he was defeated.'

'Tell me about your husband.'

'Well, I was twenty-three when I met him. He gave me a very nice home, a lovely daughter, Sophie, a place in society. What more could I want?'

He was watching her shrewdly as he asked, 'Tell me — I don't know.'

'Nothing. Nothing at all.'

It was said too brightly to deceive him. He pressed the point. 'Well, you want his complete recovery from his illness.'

'Naturally. He is recovering.'

'Without you beside him?'

'He's … well enough for me to leave him now. I have to work. There are distractions with illness in the house. I need to be free of them.'

George Dugdale smiled through his cigar smoke, which he wafted away from her. 'And instead, you're being distracted by me and my impertinent questions. But you must allow me the simple joy of being intrigued by you. I've always found conjugal loyalty a most appealing quality in women.'

'Are you married, Mr Dugdale?'

'My wife died five years ago. Our son is twenty now. He's at Balliol. Have some more Cointreau?'

'No, thank you. I really think I should be getting back.'

Instead of summoning the waiter, he reached over the table and put his hand on one of hers.

'Diana … if I may call you Diana? Let us return to the Bentinck and discuss our relationship in private.'

'Our relationship? Really, Mr Dugdale, you're rushing ahead of me. I wasn't aware there was any relationship.'

'Two people dining alone together at the Savoy usually implies some sort of a relationship.'

'Well, you must forgive my innocence. If I'd thought that by accepting your kind offer assumptions were being made…'

He said earnestly. 'Good heavens, not at all. I simply have to tell you that you've captured my heart. It was never assumed. It's happened, and I can't conceal it.'

Flustered, Diana protested, 'But it's impossible! Excuse me, but I really should like to get back to my painting.'

'Pussy and her moralising,' he said without sarcasm, withdrawing his hand. He smiled. 'Forgive me. Widowers are prone to idiotic passions, you know. You're quite right to treat them with the utmost circumspection.'

'It's not that,' she said, not wishing to wound his feelings and feeling genuinely complimented by this well-placed, intelligent, good-looking man. 'I'm touched. I'm only sorry that you've misjudged me. I'm truly not accustomed to … adventures.'

'So I sense,' he said, signalling for the waiter at last. 'But if we aren't to be lovers, will you accept instead my humble and sincere offer of friendship?'

She smiled gratitude and relief. 'Yes. That I *would* like, Mr Dugdale.'

'George, please — Diana.'

It required only two days for his friendship with her to take tangible shape. He came into her room in the morning to find her at her easel as usual. The room was rapidly assuming the appearance of a regular studio. Diana wore her rough, stained working overall. Her position by the brightness of the window rendered her expression hard to discern; in any case, Dugdale was too preoccupied with his news to notice a certain puffiness around her eyes.

'I laid them out on Hurst's table and he expressed immediate approval,' he announced triumphantly. 'I knew he would. He thinks it will make a splendid book, and he sees a whole series. He wants to meet you. I've arranged for the three of us to lunch at the Savoy on Monday. I take it you won't mind breaking off for that?'

Her voice faltered a little as she said, 'No … no. That's wonderful.' But there was no joy or enthusiasm in her tone.

'I shall act as your lawyer and get you a suitable advance payment,' he said. 'A few hundred, without a doubt.'

To his surprise she suddenly subsided into a chair and burst into tears. He hurried across to crouch beside her and ask soothingly and with real concern what was the matter. Unable to speak, she indicated a letter. He picked it up and read it silently, then frowned over the signature.

'Joseph Stewart?'

'Our land agent. He's been dealing with all the bills and correspondence since Harry's illness. He wouldn't have told me if he could have avoided it, I'm sure, but this wretched Coulter means to bring a court case.'

'Did you know Harry had gambling debts?'

'Yes. But not the size of them.'

'I assume the estate is mortgaged.'

Diana nodded miserably. 'When we had no son, my husband felt it wouldn't be worth perpetuating anyway. He said we might as well enjoy it.'

'What do you do for income?'

She gestured wildly towards the easel. 'This is our income. That's why I'm here, trying to work in peace. But I simply can't work fast enough to pay the household bills.'

With a determined effort she stopped herself crying again. George Dugdale was getting out his cheque book and fountain pen. He began to write. Diana saw her name and exclaimed, 'No, you mustn't! I couldn't accept anything from you — four hundred pounds?'

George calmly tore out the cheque and forced it into her hand, which he squeezed upon it. 'See it as my investment in our animal friends,' he smiled.

She still protested. 'I'd rather ask James Rosslyn for help. He's a family friend. I'll never be able to pay you this much back.'

'Yes, you will. You'll find your work worth far more than that in the long run. Leave that to Hurst and me. Besides, you could regard it as a seal on our special friendship. I … pressed my claim too early, the other day. It's a failing of mine. I see something I want and I go for it. I lack patience. Two days have passed now, and I've had ample time to reflect. Please don't think I'm trying to take advantage of your distress — of what I've just learned — or that I'm breaking our bargain, our pact of friendship. But love grows out of friendship, doesn't it? They spring from the same root. So I want to offer you help, protection … and love, for as long as you want them.'

Clutching his forgotten cheque, Diana stared at him long and hard. Then thankfully, willingly, she let herself lean against him, and when his arm stole round her, raised her mouth to meet his.

'It's incredible!' Sir James Rosslyn fumed.

He had come round on Sunday afternoon, hoping to find Diana free for a walk in St James's Park, and been told by a matter-of-fact Louisa that she was spending the weekend with 'Mr Duggy' at his cottage in the New Forest.

'Oh, come on, Sir James,' Louisa said. 'Cheer up! It's only a weekend in the country.'

'Only…!'

'Best thing could've happened, you ask me. Her husband's no use to her. She's working her heart out here to keep things going, and she needs friends. I know. I've been through it all meself, and it's no joke, I can tell you.'

But he was in no mood for her cocky banter. 'Mrs Trotter, I don't think you quite understand the implications of this … this affair. We're about to fight a General Election. If there should be any divorce scandal just now…'

'Who said anything about a divorce?' she retorted, refusing to be put down. 'Just a bit of fun, that's all.'

Sir James sighed. 'My dear Mrs Trotter, you don't know the lady at all if you believe that. She's not the sort to indulge in "fun", as you call it. If that cunning George Dugdale's made his impression on her, as I feared from the start he was out to do, then there will be no going back after this weekend. I fear the worst.'

'Well, if the news does get out, it won't be from behind these walls, I can promise you that,' Louisa said.

The couple had scarcely returned from an idyllic stay in the New Forest cottage before Sir James Rosslyn sought out Dugdale and charged him angrily with putting the Liberal Party's reputation at risk. George retorted spiritedly that the election result was a foregone conclusion, in their favour, and that it would take a scandal of immense proportions to make the slightest effect on the voters. He scoffed at a warning that he might be compromising his own chance of a Cabinet post. With supreme self-confidence, he insisted that he fully expected 'something' at the Board of Trade, come what might.

'Anyway,' he went on, 'who's going to hear about Diana and me? And if they do, who'll have told them? Not you, I hope, my dear James.'

'Of course not. But you can't blame me if Campbell Bannerman learns of it somehow else.'

'Well, that's my risk. Anyway, I'm not the only one who enjoys a little discreet private life, you know. Look at Lloyd George … Asquith … You don't tell me CB will give them the order of the boot for it.'

'No man,' Sir James said primly, 'however brilliant he may consider himself to be, is greater than the party he stands for.'

'Oh, damn the party and such arrant nonsense. All men are greater than the party, unless they choose to be its lapdog, which I'm afraid you tend to be, James. It's individuals who count in the end — warts and all. Oh, I'm sorry, I don't mean to offend you. Sit down and have a drink. We've known each other far too long for this sort of wrangling.'

Sir James accepted sorrowfully. He was sincere in his attitude to the matter, but he knew himself to be no match for the stubborn determination of George Dugdale in pursuit of something he meant to achieve.

'Anyway,' George was saying, as he poured sherry, 'she'll be along in a minute. She'll be pleased to find you here. She talked about you a great deal. You've been a steadfast friend, and by God she must have needed one.'

'You know, then — about the marriage?'

'Oh yes, it all came tumbling out. I've no doubt she was to blame for some of the problems. She's not an easy woman — too highly strung. But I find her adorable. I'm besotted with her.'

The object of his adoration arrived just then. She smiled a little nervously at the sight of Sir James getting to his feet. Dugdale put his arm round her and led her over.

'My darling,' he greeted her fearlessly, 'come and have a glass of sherry with your old friend, who, incidentally, knows all about us.'

Her smile changed to one of relief. She asked Sir James lightly, 'What have you two been talking about, then?'

George Dugdale answered, 'The insignificance of politics.'


The publisher's luncheon at the Savoy had been the success George Dugdale had predicted, and more. He was so enthusiastic about Diana's artistic style and her outline for the book that he commissioned it on the spot, with an option on further ones. But he set a fierce deadline for the initial volume, in order, he explained, to catch the spring market.

'Can you manage it?' George asked her, as they sat side by side on his sofa back at the Bentinck afterwards.

'I'll work day and night,' she declared. 'The only time I shall allow myself off will be the time I give you. You've changed my life — in more ways than one.' She kissed him.

'Yes, well, I shan't trespass too much on your time, anyway,' he said. 'The election's been set for January. I shall have to spend a lot of time in my constituency. After the shock of last time, the Tories will be putting everything they can into their campaign.'

'Oh, I wish I could come with you. How can I work without you near me? With you, I can achieve anything.'

He patted her thigh. 'Nonsense. You'll work all the harder. And I shall be working, too. We shan't distract one another.'

She nodded resignedly. 'I've made too many demands on you already. I can't believe my good fortune. You do love me, though?'

'I adore you.'

'And you will keep loving me? Life could never be the same again without you.'

He held her tenderly and kissed her. 'When I'm away,' he promised, 'I shall write to you every single day. You'll see how quickly the time will pass.'

She set herself a rigorous working routine, keeping up with her other commitments while devoting part of each day to the book. When January came and George did go away, she found herself able to achieve even more, working additionally in the evenings which she might otherwise have spent with him. When things were going well she often yielded to the temptation to work into the small hours, and one morning Mary came in with her breakfast to find her asleep, fully clothed, on the sofa, with pages of handwritten manuscript strewn around her.

'You haven't been to bed, madam!' she scolded, when Diana opened bleary eyes. 'You'll wear yourself out, that you will.'

But Diana was quickly wide awake, eager to seize the letter lying on the tray and rip it open.

Mary picked up a sketch. It was a heron with the unmistakable features of Merriman. She smiled at the likeness and put it down. 'Not very nice campaigning weather, madam,' she said. 'It snowed all night. I'll run you a nice hot bath, shall I?'

Diana didn't answer. She was happily absorbed in George's letter.

She received a scolding from Sir James Rosslyn, too, when he called later in the week to ask after her welfare and she showed him the pile of letters.

'Diana, you must come to your senses. There's no future in it, I tell you. You certainly can't divorce Harry, and if he hears about it and divorces you, then George's career is in ruins and you'll both be outcasts from society.'

'He says that's all rubbish.'

'That's the man's colossal vanity.'

'James,' she implored, 'will you please stop trying to make me feel guilty? Of course I don't want to hurt Harry. He isn't expected to live long, so if we must, we'll wait.'

Rosslyn gave her a pitying look. 'You think George will *marry* you? Has he proposed?'

'Not yet. He must know he can't.' She gestured towards the letters. 'But he talks about our future on nearly every page.'

'He doesn't say much about the past, though, I'll wager.'

Diana said coolly, 'That's unfair of you, James. He's been a widower for five years. I wouldn't have expected him to have remained celibate all that time.'

'My dear, the list of women stretches back to a long time before Isobel's death. And it's a long one. The plain fact is that George Dugdale, for all that he may seem to be charming and brilliant, is nothing more than a cheap opportunist. And that's not just my view…'

'And I thought you were his friend!'

'Diana, before anything else, I am *your* friend.'

'Well, you've an extraordinary way of showing it. You're a misery and a Jeremiah, knowing my feelings and trying every trick to take away the happiness I've found. Now will you please leave me? I've a lot of work to do.'

He hesitated, then went. Diana threw aside the sketch she had begun and began to work savagely on a new one. It was of a stringy-looking buzzard, with the face of Sir James Rosslyn.

One Monday morning shortly afterwards she went out to buy more paints, pausing at the hall desk to give Starr a letter to post to George. 'Mary forgot to bring my post up this morning,' she said. 'May I have it, please?'

Starr folded his newspaper. 'I'm afraid there were no letters for you this morning, madam.'

Diana frowned. It was the first time. 'You're sure?'

'Positive, madam. I'm sorry.'

When she had gone out Starr went straight to Louisa's parlour, taking the newspaper with him. 'I thought you ought to see this, madam,' he said, pointing out a brief item of gossip. 'In view of the person involved, and the possible consequences.'

'Yeh,' she said thoughtfully. 'Go and fetch Merriman and Mary here, straight away.'

When they were assembled, and her parlour door shut, Louisa said, 'Now then, Mr Starr has just shown me a piece of tittle-tattle in this rag of his about Mr Dugdale being seen in Deauville over the weekend with a certain Mrs Monroe, a widow, and rumours of a romance between 'em.'

'Where's Deauville, ma'am?' Mary asked.

'In France. Now, I'm sure this isn't the kind of newspaper Mrs Strickland's likely to read, even by chance. She just has *The Times,* and they don't go in for this sort of thing. But it's a wonder how things like this get passed on by so-called "well-wishers", and I just want to warn you lot to do anything you can to make sure she doesn't get to know. Right?'

They agreed, and dispersed. Louisa was worried, though. She summoned her counsellor, Major Smith-Barton, separately. 'What do you make of it?' she asked.

'There's no smoke without fire, they say.'

'But he couldn't do it to her! They're like turtle doves when they're together.'

The major said, 'Funnily enough, I met one of his colleagues in the club, the other day. I mentioned Dugdale and he asked if there was any truth in a rumour about him and this Mrs Monroe. Apparently, she's got rather a reputation for this sort of thing. Married two politicians, both of whom died before they reached the Cabinet, and the jokers are saying she's looking for third time lucky.'

'Oh, blimey!' Louisa groaned. 'But it says here she's forty-eight. Makes her sound an old frump, compared with Mrs Strickland.'

'Yes, but she has money — influence.'

'Well, he's due back any day. She didn't get a letter from him this morning, so he might be on his way.'

The major said, 'According to my friend he's been seen in London once or twice while he's been "away" … at the theatre with Mrs Monroe. Rye isn't far from here, after all. Easily nip up and back again in an evening.'

'Then everyone'll know soon. D'you reckon it's any of my business to warn her? I can't stick seeing women getting hurt by men.'

'It's a tricky one,' the major said thoughtfully. 'It would soften the blow a bit.'

'Yeh. Once old Sir Rosy gets wind of it you can bet he'll be running round here like a shot. I'd better tell her. Kinder in the long run.'

She did, taking the newspaper item with her as corroboration. Diana was shocked, and cried at first, but quickly pulled herself together and insisted stubbornly that the whole thing was just scandal-mongering, with the election coming up. And even as Louisa was talking to her, Mary came in with a letter by a later post. Diana opened it eagerly. It was from George, saying he would be back at the Bentinck that very evening and was longing to see her again. He asked her to order dinner at eight in her room.

A little before eight he breezed into the hotel, greeting Louisa and Merriman cheerfully in the hall. He ran up to his own room to wash and change, then went straight along to Diana's. He found her, looking radiant in her dinner gown, and embraced her ardently. Nothing in her manner betrayed the lurking doubt which underlaid her delight at his return.

'I've missed you so much,' he said, as they drank sherry. 'I'll be glad when this damned election's over. How've you been? Have you worked well? I can't wait to see what you've done.'

'It's all over there in a folder,' she said. 'After dinner, though. I've missed you, too, darling. Here, I've bought you a welcome-home present.'

She handed over a little leather case. He found in it a pair of silver cufflinks, engraved with his initials.

'They're for good luck at the election, too,' she added.

'Oh, but they're splendid! Thank you so much, my angel. I shall wear them on polling day.' He kissed her again and said, 'I'm sorry, I've nothing for you. There simply wasn't time.'

Merriman was in attendance throughout the dinner. At last he was dismissed, with their compliments to Mrs Trotter for a superb meal.

'Much better,' George sighed contentedly. 'What a difference from those provincial hotels.'

'And Deauville?' asked Diana, who had had to contain herself throughout dinner.

He looked surprised, but didn't lose his smile. 'How did you know I'd been to Deauville?'

'It was in a newspaper. I'd have thought you'd have sent me a postcard.'

'D'you know, I wrote one and forgot to post the damned thing. I found it in my pocket, back in England.'

'Why did you go?' she asked, trying to sound casual.

'I went because I was invited. One of my disgustingly rich constituents has a steam yacht. It was only for two days and it would have been impolitic to refuse. I enjoyed it, actually. A rest from speechifying.'

'The newspaper hinted at a romance with a Mrs Monroe — I suppose she is your "disgustingly rich" constituent. I paid no attention, of course.'

He laughed. 'A romance with Dorothy? Good heavens!'

He did not manage it convincingly enough, though. She knew from his forced laugh that he was putting on an act. Also, no two days had elapsed without a letter from him. He must have written one and left it with someone in England to post while he was away. This calculated deception brought back her worst fears with a rush.

'George,' she said, 'please don't. You have to tell me sometime.'

His smile gradually faded. After a long pause he said, 'Yes, I suppose I do. I can't deceive you, because I'm too fond of you. The newspaper was right in the main, only "romance" is hardly the word. I've known Dorothy Monroe for years. A romance is something special. Something you and I had.'

'"Had"?'

'Look, believe me, Diana, my feelings for you were genuine. They still are. I'd much rather spend my life with you, but we have to be realistic, don't we? The truth is, we're both victims of circumstance.'

'Victims? Yes! You took me like a dog picks up a bone. Didn't you realise that you changed my life? That I could never return…'

'Oh, good heavens, that's not true. I helped you back on your feet, that's all. You're strong now. You're independent. You have a book to write, a belief in yourself again.'

'I loved you! You opened my eyes to possibilities I'd never dreamed of. You were the finest man I'd met. I worshipped your mind, your body. I trusted you.'

'Absurd! I am a man … with frailties…'

'Yes, you are. That was my mistake.' She was too furious to cry.

He made a placatory move towards her, but she shrank away.

He floundered, 'I'm sorry … truly sorry you should feel like this about me. I thought … I assumed you realised that sooner or later…' He got to his feet. 'Well, I shan't forget you.' He gave her a farewell smile, and gestured towards her folder. 'Or my friends in the forest.'

Only when he had gone did she cry — dreadfully.

The next morning a red-eyed Diana told Mary she would be leaving the Bentinck that day, and requested her bill to be prepared. Louisa brought it up herself while Diana was packing.

'So it was true, was it?' she asked.

Diana, almost unnaturally calm, simply nodded.

'You'll fight him?' Louisa said.

Diana shook her head. 'He's not worth fighting.'

''Course he is! He's rotten, and the whole world should know what he's done to you. Make him an example to the rest of his kind. Besides, we don't want *him* running the bloomin' country!'

'It was my fault, Mrs Trotter. I was blind, selfish…'

'Oh, come on…!'

'Anyway, I've no weapons to fight him with.'

'You've got all those letters, haven't you? Look, Lord Northcliffe comes here. He's a pal of mine. He'll know what to do with 'em.'

'Why should I hurt him?' Diana retorted, to Louisa's surprise. 'He was right, in a way. He did help me. He found me a publisher. He set me on my feet. I've much to be grateful for.'

'What?'

'He lent me money, too.'

'For Gawd's sake,' Louisa cried, 'how much?'

'Four hundred pounds. I shall earn it from my first book and pay him back. But now I must return home, to my husband and my daughter. I've neglected them. I've been disloyal to them … and George needs Mrs Monroe. As for the letters, the last thing I shall do before I leave here, Mrs Trotter, is burn them all.'

She did; and left. That same day George Dugdale left again for Rye, to do his final canvassing before the General Election. To his surprise, Louisa presented him with his bill, fully made up. He raised his eyebrows but, without comment, felt in his breast pocket for his cheque book.

'You won't need that,' she told him.

'I beg your pardon?'

'You've paid already. In fact, I owe you some. Seventy pounds ten shillings, to be precise. The balance on what you lent Mrs Strickland. I'm relievin' you of that obligation.'

'But this is absurd!' he protested. 'It was a private matter.'

'Yeh, well it's my business now. So's you can wipe the whole slate clean between you.'

After a long pause, Dugdale said, 'What … terrible tales has she been telling you, Mrs Trotter?'

'She said nothing terrible, Mr Dugdale. She stuck up for you. You won't have no trouble with her. She's a saint, and you're lucky. There's plenty of others you couldn't have done this to and got away with it.'

'I see,' he said, with something approaching humility. 'Goodbye, Mrs Trotter. I've been most comfortable here.'

'Goodbye. And I'd prefer it if you didn't come here again. Not even if you get to be bleedin' Prime Minister.'


The General Election proved a triumph for the Liberal Party. The evening following it, the Bentinck Hotel resounded again to an even greater celebratory roar.

'Hurry up, Mr Merriman!' cried Mary into the dispense. 'They're bellowing out for more champagne.'

'As quick as I can,' the old hand groaned.

'You'd never believe it,' she said to Starr. 'That Mr Dugdale's up there as well, with his fiancée, Mrs Monroe.'

'There'll be a fair old rumpus if Mrs Trotter finds out, won't there?'

'What? She's there, in the thick of it.'

'I tell you,' Merriman said, emerging with his loaded tray, 'hotels is like hospitals. They're all bodies. You do your best for 'em, but once you get your feelings involved…' He staggered on his way.

'You lose out on tips, eh?' Starr said. He looked down at Fred. 'Mrs Trotter's learning, me old son. Isn't she?'

# CHAPTER FIVE

A few weeks later, Louisa went away on holiday. As always, she went reluctantly, preferring activity to idleness. She rarely did absent herself, and then only when practically ordered to by Lord Haslemere, who would visit town briefly, notice signs of strain in her features and manner, and, after long argument, pack her off to Margate or somewhere, even if only for a few days. He never suggested taking her away himself. Their brief romance was never referred to now, and that aspect of their relationship dead and buried.

This time she had been cajoled further afield — not by Charlie, whom she had not seen since the beginning of the year, but by a French count with a château in the champagne country. She could sense herself that she needed a rest, and the count was an elderly charmer who stayed at the Bentinck whenever he visited London. Louisa knew that he had a countess and several sons and daughters at the chateau. She felt she would at least be left unpestered, so accepted.

'Wish I hadn't,' she grumbled to Mary on the morning of her departure, the count having gone ahead a week earlier. 'Can't stick holidays. I'm all on edge, and worst of all, when I come back, everything's always in a mess.' She was standing on the pavement in front of the hotel.

'That's not fair!' Mary had the spirit to retort. 'We look after everything, don't we, Major?'

'Do our best, eh?' Smith-Barton grinned. 'Don't worry, Mrs Trotter. I'll keep an eye on things, don't you know?'

'Well … laundry maid, don't forget. There's two applicants coming tomorrow from that agency. And look after Miss Hayward, the bishop's daughter. She's been a regular for years, but she always fusses.'

'I know,' Mary said firmly. 'We'll be quite all right. Now, you'll miss your train unless…'

After a last despairing glance up at her hotel, Louisa allowed herself to be driven away by the major in the smart new hotel 'bus. It might have been a tumbril taking her to execution, to judge from her face. Preoccupied with herself, she had no reason to notice a slightly blowsy, poorly dressed young woman, who had been leaning on a bicycle within earshot of the conversation.

Louisa had barely been gone ten minutes before Miss Hayward, a brisk and domineering fifty, and her sour, pious maid Morgan, came marching down to the hall desk where Starr, in his porter's uniform, was checking advance bookings with Mary.

'I want to see Mrs Trotter,' Miss Hayward demanded.

'She's gone away, madam,' Starr explained. 'Can I or Miss Philips help?'

'My maid has found a cockroach in her bedroom. Show them, Morgan.'

The stringy maid stepped forward and, with an expression accentuating her usual distaste for everything, opened a small box at arm's length and placed it on the counter. Starr peered close.

'It's a big fellow,' he said interestedly. 'See that, Mary?'

With more tact, Mary said, 'I'm very sorry, Miss Hayward.'

The bishop's daughter sniffed. 'What concerns me is that cockroaches are more usually found in kitchens.'

'Oh, not in ours, madam. Our kitchens are spotless. You're welcome to come down and see.'

'I don't think so, thank you,' Miss Hayward replied loftily, as if she had never deigned to enter a kitchen in her life. 'Come along, Morgan. Harrods.'

They swept out. Mary went off into Louisa's room. Starr threw the dead cockroach, in its box, into his waste-paper basket. As he straightened up he found Merriman approaching, carrying a letter.

'For you,' the old waiter said. 'A young woman left it at the back door just now.'

Starr, frowning, opened the letter and read its scrawled message. His frown deepened. Then he asked Merriman to look after the desk and Fred while he just popped out for a few minutes.

His steps took him to a small public house, some fifty yards round the nearest corner, mostly frequented by servants, soldiers and small tradesmen. It was fairly full, and he had to glance around until he saw the person he was seeking. It was the young woman bicyclist who had overheard Louisa's parting words to the major and Mary. Starr went to where she was sitting at a long table with two glasses of stout in front of her. She smiled up tentatively, but he didn't smile in return.

'Hello, Joey,' she greeted him. 'Bought you a glass of your old favourite.' She indicated the stout. 'See — I don't forget. You're lookin' all right. Smart uniform.'

He sat down reluctantly, wanting to keep their conversation subdued. 'What you doing here, Lizzie? What d'you want?'

'See you, that's all. No law against it, is there? Hard to find, though, you were. Tramped all over London. Still be lookin', if I hadn't met Corporal Philpott — remember, the one with the big ears? He's a baker's roundsman now, and he knew where you was.'

He said suspiciously, 'I thought we agreed ... not to meet again.'

'Is that all you can say, Joey? Didn't you never think of me — if I was alive or dead, even? I've thought of you.'

'Evidently, or you wouldn't be here now. What're you after, Lizzie?'

She looked at him levelly. She was in her thirties, some few years younger than he. Her face bore vestiges of a wild beauty and her figure was still good, but her forehead and neck were lined and her hands were rough, with dirty nails. Her clothing was far from new and not well tended.

'I want a job,' she answered simply.

'A job? Well, I can't give you one.'

'You could help. Must be somethin' in that hotel — cleaning, scrubbin' ... I'm not proud. Please, Joey. I'm desperate. It's not been easy ... on me own.'

He hadn't touched the drink she had bought him. He said flintily, 'I don't believe you've been on your own, Lizzie. Not you.'

Her eyes glittered resentfully. 'I have! More often than not, anyway. I'm not a whore.'

'All right, calm down, calm down,' he urged her, glancing anxiously around.

She insisted, more quietly, 'I'm not askin' for money, Joey. I ain't got none, but I'm not askin' for it. Just want a job and a bit of respect, like you've got.'

'There's other jobs,' he pointed out.

'Yeh, I've had some of 'em. Makin' trousers in a sweatshop. Twelve hours a day for a lousy shilling. Barmaid in Stepney.

That wasn't bad, but the landlord was. Joey, there was a time when you thought I was worth more'n that sort of thing.'

'I don't want to talk about that,' he said firmly. 'It's finished. I've got my life settled now and I don't want you barging your way back into it. I'm sorry, Lizzie, but you'll have to look elsewhere.'

She looked him full in the eyes and asked, 'Do they *know* about you at the Bentinck, Joey? Tell 'em all your past, did you?'

As has been said, Starr had been more than reticent upon that subject when first interviewed by Louisa. And ever since he had maintained his inscrutable pose, volunteering nothing about himself to anyone and carefully avoiding answering the occasional probings of Merriman, who sensed a fellow old soldier in Starr, but couldn't win so much as an admission that he had ever been one.

'Bitch!' he said to the watching woman.

'Yeh,' she sighed. 'That's what life can make you, innit?'

'Do your worst,' he replied, trying to call her bluff. 'Go and tell 'em, then. It won't get you a job, though. Anyway, there isn't one going.'

'There is. I heard that woman, just before she got on the 'bus. Talking about some laundry maids coming to be seen. I could do that.'

'No.'

She changed her tone, not to wheedling, but to what Starr thought he sensed was genuine desperation. 'Oh, please, Joey. Just till I get on my feet. Then I'll move on. I won't make you no trouble. Promise.'

He looked at her for some moments before replying uncertainly, 'You won't breathe a word?'

'Honest.'

There was a further pause before he said, 'I can't … fix it for you. You'd have to get it on merit, against the others.'

She smiled again. 'You could give me a reference at least. Thanks, Joey. Drink your stout, love.'

She placed her hand over his on the table. He gave her a little smile at last, picked up the glass, and drank.


Mary Philips interviewed the applicants in the laundry room itself, a below-stairs apartment with a stone floor sloping gently towards a gutter and drain, a boiler, a row of tubs, two mangles, an ironing table and various shelves and cupboards holding piles of folded white linen. The first two women were disappointments: one too old and slow, the other young but clearly not mentally fitted to do more than scrub floors or carry coals. Lizzie, by contrast, made a good impression. She had tidied her hair and cleaned herself up. She spoke respectfully and confidently.

'After me husband died I had to get work where I could,' she explained to Mary. 'I never worked in a hotel before, but I expect it's the same as washin' and ironin' in your own home, innit? Only, like a bigger family.'

'I suppose it is,' Mary smiled.

Lizzie went on, 'Sort out all the different things into piles, do I? White linen, body linen, collars…'

'That's it. How would you remove an ink stain, say?'

'Good rub with soap and water?' Lizzie suggested hopefully, not knowing.

'No. You need salts of sorrel for ink marks.'

'Ah, well, soon pick it all up, if you don't mind me askin' questions, miss.'

Mary's mind was almost made up. 'And you say you're acquainted with Mr Starr, Mrs Talbot?'

'Oh, some years. We hadn't bumped into each other for ever such a long time, though. Mr Starr was my late husband's best friend. Sergeants together. He was with my husband when he was killed. Brought his things back for me. I'm sure he'll speak for me, miss.'

'All right,' Mary told her. 'We'll take that for granted, then. The job's yours.'

'I'm ever so grateful, miss. There's … no chance of livin' in, is there?'

'I'm afraid not. Have you far to come?'

'From the East End. But I've got me bike.'

'Good. Well, the wages are fifteen shillings a week and all meals. Is that satisfactory?'

'Thank you, miss. Want me to start now, as I'm here?'

'If you could I'd be grateful. We are rather behind. There are some aprons over here.'

Lizzie took off her coat and hat and hung them up, donned an apron, and set to with a will.

A little later Mrs Cochrane looked round the door and saw Lizzie ironing busily. 'Hello, dear,' she smiled. 'I'm the cook, Mrs Cochrane. We're having our tea in a minute. You'll come and join us?'

'Ta,' Lizzie accepted pleasantly. 'Just finish these last things first.'

When she went into the servants' hall she found Mrs Cochrane, her kitchen maid and Merriman seated at the table, drinking tea and eating bread and jam. Introductions were made and Merriman lapsed into munching silence again. Mrs Cochrane passed Lizzie her cup and said, 'Mary — Miss Philips — says you're a widow, Mrs Talbot.'

'Yeh. Call me Lizzie, please.'

'Very well, dear. I'm a widow, too.'

'Hard life, eh?'

'Yes. Mr Cochrane's been gone fourteen years come August. He went in for a bathe at Margate, straight after a big dinner. I told him it would be bad… Still, my children have been good to me. You got any children, Lizzie?'

'No. Only married six months.'

'Oh, what a shame!'

'Yeh. Tall, handsome, my Jack was. Big shoulders. Lovely man.'

'And he was killed fighting with Mr Starr, I believe.'

'Side by side, at the battle of Omdurman.'

Starr entered at that moment, in time to hear the reference to him. Even Merriman shed his deafness in the presence of some interesting information at last.

Lizzie smiled at Starr and patted Fred. 'That's a nice dog, Mr Starr,' she said. 'You always was fond of animals, wasn't you? Remember in Malta, that big white rabbit we had that John looked after?'

'Didn't know you was in Malta, Mr Starr,' Merriman said.

Starr said nothing, but Lizzie prattled on. 'Yeh. That's where they were. Rifle Brigade. Second battalion. Before they went to Egypt.'

'You was in the Rifle Brigade?' Merriman tried again, impressed.

'Quartermaster sergeant,' Lizzie answered, smiling at Starr, who shot her a warning look.

'Kept that a dark secret,' Merriman was going on.

Again it was Lizzie who replied. 'Well, not all men like to boast about their fightin' days, do they, Mr Starr?'

He crammed bread into his mouth, and was further saved from having to speak by the entry of Mary, with a list of guests due to leave and talk of arrangements to be made accordingly.

That evening, Starr ushered Fred into their bedroom. The dog barked once and growled. Starr was astonished to see Lizzie in her underclothes, holding her dress.

'What the hell…!' he exclaimed, shutting the door hurriedly and silencing Fred, who by now had recognised Lizzie anyway.

'Just had a bath along the passage,' she explained. 'Ain't got one where I live. It's all right, I asked Mrs Cochrane. Smell … real soap. I feel human again.'

She extended a slender arm. Even in his shocked state of indignation he could see that her body was attractively moulded. He ignored the arm and said, 'This is my room. You've no right in here.'

'Is it?' Lizzie replied with apparent innocence. 'I thought it was a spare.'

True, Starr had made little imprint on himself on his surroundings. Most of his belongings were out of sight. But the dog basket beside the bed was obvious enough.

'Well, hurry up and get out,' he said curtly. 'Hope no one saw you come in.'

Lizzie went on dressing. 'Don't be hasty with me, Joey,' she said. 'I've had a hard day. Worked like a slave in that laundry room. Made a good impression, have I?'

'Not on me, you haven't. Too much blabbermouth. You promised…'

'Well, how was I to know you'd told 'em nothin' at all? There's *some* bits you're not ashamed of.'

'It suited me to tell 'em nothing. Build up again from scratch. A new man. Now you've come and the questions'll start. I'm not as easy a liar as you are. They'll catch me out, and then I'm done for.'

She had got her dress fastened now. She looked at herself in his small shaving mirror. 'Sorry, Joey, I won't say another word, even if they ask me.' With a coquettish twirl round to face him she said gaily, 'Kept me figure, you got to admit. Bloomin' miracle. Fancy takin' me for a drink?'

'Can't. I'm on duty.'

'Oh, well, see you tomorrow, then,' Lizzie said, clearly disappointed.

'Where are you living?' Starr asked, unbending a little.

'Whitechapel. It's quite quick on me bike, really.'

He asked hesitantly, 'Lizzie … you living on your own, are you?'

She smiled. ''Course I'm on me own. One room. Just like this. Goodnight, Joey.'

She went out quickly, closing the door. Starr sat on his bed, absently running his fingers through Fred's fur, lost in thought and memories.


Next morning, he entered the servants' hall to find Mrs Cochrane clucking over Lizzie, who was seated on a chair, wincing as the cook applied a compress to what was revealed to be a nasty black eye.

'Young thug gave her it on her way to work,' Mrs Cochrane explained.

'Yeh,' Lizzie confirmed, quite cheerfully. 'About fifteen, he was. There was a gang of 'em, pummelin' some poor little runt. Florence Nightingale goes to 'is rescue and gets this for her pains.'

'The sooner you're out of the East End, the better,' the cook told her. 'Don't you agree, Mr Starr? No place for a poor young woman on her own.'

Lizzie's good eye caught Starr's look. She managed a wink. He didn't return it or answer Mrs Cochrane's remark, but later in the day he did come down to the laundry room and invite

Lizzie to have a drink with him when he came off duty that evening.

They went to the pub of their first encounter. Fred did not accompany them. He had been left in Merriman's care. Lizzie's eye had really blackened by now and was nearly closed. She looked round and giggled.

'Gettin' some funny looks,' she said. 'They must think you're my old man and it was you done this.' She pointed to the eye.

Starr smiled. He was more relaxed in her presence now. She could feel it. She said, 'We oughter gone somewhere else, I suppose. Someone you know might come in. Bad for your reputation.'

He was genuinely touched that she should have given the matter a thought.

'Anyone who knows me knows I live in and I'm not married,' he replied easily. 'Does it hurt?'

'No. Wait till I see that copper-nob kid again, though. I'll put one on him first.'

'Rest of you's all right — what I've seen,' he surprised her by saying.

'Thanks, Joey,' she said. 'That's nice of you.'

'I'm taking you home,' he said suddenly. 'You're not fit to bike with one eye shut. We'll get the 'bus.'

'I'm all right, Joey, thanks,' she said hastily. 'Really.' But he was draining his glass and getting up. 'Come on,' he ordered. 'I'm hungry. We'll get some jellied eels.'

He failed to recognise her reluctance as she got up and obediently left the public house with him. As they walked along she said, 'I don't want you to see my home. It's not nice.'

'I don't care about that.'

She had to give in. 'Well, if you must. But I warn you…' She cheered up. 'I've got some halibut, if it hasn't been nicked. How about that, fried?'

Starr licked his lips and grinned. 'Quite fancy a bit of that.' When they were well clear of the vicinity of the Bentinck he took her arm and held it all the way to the 'bus terminal at Piccadilly Circus.

The room proved to be as unsavoury as she had warned him it was. It was in a noisy and noisome tenement building, a small, low-ceilinged little room with a bare floor and stained walls, a rickety table, one plain chair and two fruit boxes, a couch-bed with a ragged coverlet, and very little else. The hissing gas jet revealed nothing of feminine comfort.

Lizzie fried the halibut on a small old gas cooker. Starr stared about with distaste. 'How long've you been here?' he asked.

'All winter. Lucky to get it?

He wandered about, eyeing the marks where bugs had been squashed and flies swatted. A few pans lay on an open shelf. He spotted something else there, too.

'What's this?' he demanded. His sharp tone made her turn. He was holding up a mug containing a shaving brush and a stick of shaving soap.

Lizzie merely shrugged and turned back to her cooking. Starr looked round more keenly. On instinct, he stooped and looked under the bed. A bundle of clothing lay there. He dragged it out. It was a man's jacket and trousers.

'Might have guessed!' he said bitterly.

Lizzie had looked round again. She said urgently, 'No, Joey, it's not that. I don't know whose they are — honest. I have to share the room.'

'*Have* to?'

'It's the truth. Ask the landlord. Three bob a week I have to pay for sharin'. Bloody swizz!'

'Who with?' he asked, deeply suspicious.

'Don't ask me. It changes. Sometimes a man, sometimes a woman. We have it in shifts. We don't see each other. It's the rule. Now you know why I come to find you. Sooner I can get out, the better.'

'Same *bed*?'

'There ain't another, is there? Anyway,' she grinned, 'I took me own sheets in to the Bentinck this morning and did 'em with the rest of the wash.' She indicated the bundle she had carried on their way home. 'At least we got clean sheets tonight.' Her grin went and she looked at him seriously. 'Will you stay, Joey?' she asked. 'Face is a bit of a mess, but the rest of me's all right.'

She stepped towards him, holding out her hands. He took them impulsively and pulled her towards him. Their lips met in a long kiss. The halibut sizzled unheeded in its pan.

Merriman took Fred out for his night rounds, then took him along to Starr's room. 'There you are, Fred,' he said, pointing to the basket on the floor. The animal stood looking questioningly up at him. 'He'll not be long now,' Merriman said. 'Master'll soon be back.'

He went to his own room. He was too deaf to be woken an hour or two later, and again as dawn was breaking, by outbursts of whines and a low, keening howling. It was the first time Fred had ever been apart from Starr's presence for a whole night.

'Are you quite sure, Miss Hayward?' Major Smith-Barton was asking.

He was facing the truly irate bishop's daughter in Louisa's parlour, to which Mary had summoned him upon having heard what Miss Hayward had to say. This time it was no mere complaint. It was serious.

'Of course I'm sure,' came the answer. 'I'm not in the habit of making false accusations of theft. I think it's absolutely disgraceful.'

'Won't you sit down, please, madam?' the major suggested tactfully. 'I should like to hear the details for myself, if I may.'

'The police will have to be informed, of course,' she startled Mary by saying; but to both their relief she accepted the chair and told the major what she had already told Mary, while he polished his eyeglass vigorously.

'Yesterday morning I left seven pounds on my dressing table. Seven pounds exactly — shopping money. When I came back from my morning walk there were just four pounds.'

'Yesterday?' Mary said. 'Why didn't you tell us sooner?'

The major interceded smoothly, 'I'm sure Miss Hayward wanted to make quite certain before coming to the conclusion that the money really had been stolen, don't you know?'

'Exactly,' Miss Hayward agreed. 'I searched high and low. I asked Morgan if she had moved any of the money. Quite naturally, she pointed out that she had had no cause to; and that if she had, she would have moved it all, not simply three pounds of it.'

Mary said, 'But I did your room myself yesterday. Your chambermaid's away sick.'

Miss Hayward favoured her with one of her rare smiles. 'You had told me you intended to, Miss Philips. That is why I was confident enough to leave the money lying about anyway. Not that, I must say, in all my years of coming to the Bentinck, have I ever had cause to doubt the honesty of any member of the staff. It makes it all the more upsetting.'

'Quite, quite,' said Major Smith-Barton. 'I'm sure that, on Mrs Trotter's behalf, we are deeply appreciative of your remarks, dear lady. However, if I might suggest it, there is one alternative you may have overlooked. Your room is not locked, I believe. Your maid comes and goes from time to time. So, rather than any member of our staff, it could have been the private servant of a fellow guest who took your money. I wouldn't go so far as to suggest that it was an actual guest…'

'I should hope not, Major!'

'We can vouch for everyone in the hotel at present. But in one or two cases their servants are newcomers to us, and the trivial amount of the theft certainly points to someone for whom three pounds would be valuable enough to make the risk worth taking.'

Miss Hayward was looking at him with positive admiration. 'How clever!' she cried.

'Not at all,' he muttered modestly. 'Some experience of this sort of thing in the Army, don't you know? My suggestion — if I might, that is…?'

'By all means.'

'Thank you — is that you leave the matter in my hands. A few careful enquiries, rather than have police all over the place, asking awkward questions and upsetting people.'

'Yes,' Mary said. 'And the missing money will certainly be deducted from your account, Miss Hayward.'

Much mollified, the bishop's daughter thanked them both and went off. After brief consultation with Mary the major went out into the hall. Starr was on duty as usual, looking, the major noticed, unusually pale and peaky for him.

'Spot of bother, Starr,' the major confided. 'Some money taken from Miss Hayward's room — so she believes, anyway. Always unpleasant, this sort of thing. Bad feeling all round, don't you know? Then I expect it'll turn up in her handbag. Oh, by the way, Merriman was telling me you were in the Rifle Brigade.'

'Yes, sir,' Starr admitted defensively.

'Second battalion? Malta? Did you ever serve with an old friend of mine, Captain Mayhew?'

Starr's reply came instantly. 'No, Major. Never.'

'Ah. Good man. Must bring him round here sometime. You can have a chinwag.'

'I'm not much taken with chinwagging, sir,' Starr said. 'About the past, that is. Foot-forward's my motto.'

In the kitchen, Merriman, that retailer of news, said in a low voice to Mrs Cochrane, 'An old romance raised from the embers, d'you reckon? *Her* and Mr Starr.'

'Mrs Talbot? Whatever makes you say a thing like that, Mr Merriman?'

'He wasn't in his own bed last night. When I got up at six I found his poor dog whining and scratching at the door, so I went in. Not like Mr Starr to forget Fred, is it?'

The cook considered, then came down on the side of romance. 'Well, what if there is something? She deserves a bit of luck, poor thing. Losing her husband so soon.'

Merriman was musing. 'Husband Jack. Yes, now where does he fit in? Was Sergeant Starr carrying on with her before or after the Battle of Omdurman, if you get my drift?'

'You've got a wicked mind, Mr Merriman,' Mrs Cochrane blushed.

He tapped his nose on one side. 'A soldier's nose, Mrs C. There's something fishy going on, mark my words.'

His suspicions were deepened when, that evening, Starr once more asked him if he wouldn't mind giving Fred his late-night walk — adding, though, that he would be back easily by midnight. Merriman made no reference to his complete absence the previous night, and Starr volunteered nothing about it. Merriman agreed, intrigued to know what might happen next in this new game.

He was even more intrigued that evening to find Lizzie Talbot, dressed for going home, talking to the dog in his basket in the hall. 'Where's master, then?' she was asking playfully.

Merriman startled her by replying, 'Mr Starr's gone out.'

'Out? But —' She checked herself just in time from saying that she'd expected Starr to want to take her home again. He hadn't said anything to her during the day, and she had had no chance to chat with him, though they had managed to exchange an affectionate wink or two. 'Has he been gone for long?' she asked.

'All evening,' Merriman said. 'Didn't say where. Were you wanting to see him about something?'

His hopes that some further clue might be forthcoming were dashed — as, evidently, were her spirits. She just said, 'No. It's nothing,' and left by the front door, disregarding his reminder that it wasn't for staff use.

The last thing Lizzie suspected as she made her way disappointedly to what she called 'home' was that Starr had left earlier in order to race on there ahead of her. When she tiredly climbed the stairs to her room, he was lurking out of sight round the corner of the passage on to which her room gave. After she had gone in he crept to the closed door and listened. His jaw tightened when he heard her ask someone, 'What you doin' here? I might have brought *him* back again.'

A man's deep voice replied, 'We've got our story. I'm a tenant. Sharin'.'

'Yeh, but I told him we never…'

'Shut up. I came for what you've got for me, if you've got it — and you better had.'

'Can't wait, can you?' she said contemptuously. 'Here you are. Three quid. And it's the last I'm nickin' for you, so make the most of it.'

Starr heard the man chuckle. 'Three lovely nicker. There you are, my darlin' — one for you, two for me. Now come 'ere.'

'Get your paws off me. And keep your lousy quid. Keep it and get out. Go back to sea. Anywhere. I'm finished with you, Frank Corelli!'

'Gone soft, have you?' he sneered. 'Whose idea was it, anyway? Yer old lover boy. Too much for you, is he?'

Starr heard a sudden movement and an exclamation from the man. Then a loud slap and a cry from Lizzie.

'Stinkin' little whore!' the man shouted, and there was another blow. 'Whore from the gutter…!'

He got no further. Starr had burst into the room and flung himself at the man, regardless of the fact that the other was bigger and burlier than he. With the advantage of surprise, Starr bore the man to the floor, but he began to retaliate strongly. Starr sensed rather than saw Lizzie run from the room as his opponent began to get to his feet. Desperately, knowing himself about to be outclassed, Starr seized the only chair in the wretched room, raised it high, and brought it down on the other's head. It knocked him back to the ground, dazed. Starr, his eyes blazing, raised the chair once more, quite berserk now, ready to smash it down again and again.

But the fearful man on the floor saw him hesitate suddenly. A strange, far-off look had come into this wild intruder's eyes.

He lowered the chair slowly and staggered out of the room, like an automaton. Frank Corelli could have rushed him and hurled him downstairs. But his head hurt like hell and things were spinning round. He was content to lie where he was, rubbing his head and swearing.

Merriman was interested to see Starr return much earlier than he had thought he would. He looked somewhat dishevelled, and had nothing to say as he went straight past to his room.

There he sat on his bed, his happy dog's muzzle on his knee. 'Set up, we was, Fred,' he said. 'Should've learned my lesson years ago. In Malta, before your time, old son. Should've learned my bloody lesson then.'

There came a tapping at the window, urgent and almost continuous. Starr leaned over and lifted the curtain. Lizzie was outside. He could hear her saying, 'Joey! Let me in, please. Let me explain.'

'Go away,' he told her.

She shook her head. 'You've got to. I'll scream the whole place awake if you don't let me in.'

Wearily, Starr went out and unlocked the back entrance. Lizzie slipped past him and straight to his room. He glanced round, but no one was about.

Behind his closed door she pleaded, 'It was his idea, Joey. I swear it wasn't me. He said find you, get a job here, then start nickin'. I didn't want to, but he always makes me do anything he wants. The other morning — this eye — it wasn't kids. It was him. What could I do, Joey? He'd have killed me.'

'Maybe he should have.'

'I only took up with him because I was skint. I needed somebody, and he was better than nothing. Then I met you again, and I knew I wanted shut of him and the whole thing. Joey, it's *you* I want — honest.'

'You had me once. You had your chance.' He added contemptuously, 'Rifleman Williams!'

'He never meant nothing to me, Joey. You was away — maybe killed. I was scared. He took advantage…'

'They always do, don't they? Never your fault. Just a poor little victim. I loved you, Lizzie.'

'I know.'

'Worshipped you. When I met you again my mind … went back.'

Hopefully, she smiled, 'Yeh — they were good days in Malta, wasn't they? We can still do it, Joey. This hotel — I like it here. I'll go straight. We can be happy. We was the other night.'

'Yes,' he admitted. 'But I've been thinking since. I thought I'd better do some checking up, and it turned out I was right. You bring shame on me — always. You ruined me once, but not again, Lizzie. Not again. Now get out. Get back to your pimp and find somewhere else to start stealing for him.'

There was real fear in her eyes. 'No, please!' she begged. 'He'll be there … waitin'.'

'Out of my room. Go on.'

'I can't, Joey. He's waitin', I tell you. I won't. I'll scream. I'll—'

He seized her round the waist with one arm, jerked the door open with his free hand, and almost threw her across the threshold. He shut the door and rammed its bolt home. Fred came across to look up at his panting master, standing listening with his back to the door. The threatened screams never came.

Starr went back to sit on the bed. He stroked the dog, whose enquiring eyes seemed to be trying to read the meaning of it all from him.

'Gone, Fred,' was all the explanation he got. 'Gone. And good riddance.'

Lizzie didn't come to the hotel next morning. Mary asked the other staff if she had said anything to them.

Starr said heavily, 'I know all about it, miss. And Fred and me are leaving, too.'

'Oh, no!'

'You can't do that, old chap,' the major said. 'Anyway, why?'

'Private reasons, Major.'

'To do with Mrs Talbot?' Mrs Cochrane didn't hesitate to ask.

Starr nodded. 'Sorry to inconvenience you, Mary.'

The major said suspiciously, 'I think we're entitled to an explanation, Starr. Mrs Trotter certainly would be.'

Starr hesitated briefly, then said, 'It was her who took Miss Hayward's money. And since she came here at my recommendation, Fred and me think it's only right and proper that we should take our part of the blame.'

'But that's silly!' Mary protested.

'You had no part in it, did you?' the major demanded.

'No, sir.'

'Well, then. Now, come on, Starr, you just tell us all about it. We're all … friends here.'

After a further hesitation, and a doubtful glance at the women, Starr capitulated and told all his many-faceted secret. He addressed himself to the major. It was easier to confess to an officer.

'I met her in Malta — Lizzie — Mrs Talbot. Lot of 'em were after her. She chose me for some reason. Happy as larks we were.'

'But what about her husband?' Mrs Cochrane put in, preparing to become outraged.

'No such man. Just me she had, or so I thought. Common-law wife. Well, I went to Egypt and fought and came back. I'd had my suspicions of her and this Rifleman Williams before I went, but this time it was obvious. I lost my temper. The sun, Egypt, the beer… Anyway, I slammed him on the head with a rifle butt. Cracked his skull. He lived, fortunately, but I paid my dues. Court martial. Dishonourable discharge. Two years in the glasshouse. Lost my pension, *and* they took my medals away. Your friend Captain Mayhew will tell you, sir. He spoke in my defence.'

'Good heavens!' the major said, and replaced the eyeglass which had dropped out halfway through this narrative.

'Yes, sir. Eight years ago, all that was. Reasons for my reticence in matters military, Mr Merriman. And now, I think, Fred and me'll be on our way.'

'Whatever for now?' Mary asked.

'Pride, miss. All right while nobody knew. Now it'll be common gossip…'

'It certainly will not!' Mrs Cochrane said, glaring at the others for their confirmation. 'We've gossiped enough about you because you kept so secret. Made up all sorts of things, haven't we, Mr Merriman?'

The old man nodded and came over to shake Starr's hand. 'As one military man to another, Mr Starr, you've my word there'll be nothing said.'

'And mine, too,' the major said, also shaking hands. The women chimed in their support.

But Starr said, 'Mrs Trotter'll never keep us on.'

'Mrs Trotter will never know,' the major answered firmly. 'That's a further promise.'

'Well…' Starr said doubtfully. He looked down at Fred. Fred looked up at him, showing the whites of yearning eyes. 'Oh, well, we'll see how it goes, eh?'

They dispersed about their duties. Starr went off to his room to change back into the uniform he had taken off when he had resolved to leave. While he was gone two big men came into the hall. One was a police constable, but when the major approached them it was the other who asked, 'Are you by any chance the proprietor or manager of this hotel, sir?'

'No, no. The actual proprietor's away at the moment. But I have a sort of official … er… Can I help you, sir?'

'Chief Inspector Land, sir. Scotland Yard. If there's somewhere we may speak privately, please? Oh, and I should also like to speak to a Mr Joseph Starr who I believe is employed here?

'He'll be along in a few moments,' the major said. 'Just changing into his uniform.'

Starr arrived at that moment. The major ushered the party into Louisa's parlour, where Mary was sitting at the desk, and made the introductions. The Chief Inspector said, 'I understand you've recently had a laundry woman working here, by the name of Mrs Talbot.'

'Yes, sir,' Mary said. 'She hasn't turned up today, though.'

'No,' the policeman said. He referred to a notebook. 'Mrs Talbot, or Lizzie Starr, or Mrs Frank Corelli, and —' he turned to Starr — 'really named Mrs Joseph Starr. Your wife.'

'Not legally,' Starr replied. 'Common-law. Years ago.'

The officer nodded. 'I understand you haven't been living together as man and wife. Mr Starr, could you tell me when you last saw her?'

'Yes, sir. Last night.' He paused, then added, 'When she finished work. About half past six.'

'Did she go straight home, do you know?' He was watching Starr keenly.

'I couldn't say, sir,' Starr lied. 'Has … something happened?'

'I'm afraid I have to tell you that she's dead. Her body was taken out of the river by Wapping Steps in the early hours of this morning. We've reason to believe she either jumped from a bridge — or was pushed. There was a lot of bruising about her face and body.'

Starr said grimly, 'The man you want is Frank Corelli, sir.'

The policeman said, 'We know him of old. I'm afraid, though, Mr Starr, I must ask you to come and identify the body, please, and perhaps you would give us your statement at the same time.'

'I'll be glad to, sir. Poor Lizzie. A victim to the last.'

'Do you know any reason she might have had for taking her own life?'

'A lot of reasons,' Starr said, almost inaudibly. 'Years of 'em.'

He nodded to Mary, who was crying, and the major, and went away with the policeman. He was back on duty by lunchtime.


'Hello Mary, Starr,' Louisa said, as she breezed in through the front door a couple of days later. 'Hello, Major. Good to be back. Chased all round the vineyards, I was, the old devil. Anything been happenin' here?'

They were all ready for her. 'Nothing to speak of, Mrs Trotter,' the major answered. 'Very quiet, really, don't you know? Miss Hayward has gone. There have been three arrivals.'

'Get the new laundry woman, all right, Mary?'

Mary swallowed. 'Yes — well, we had one for a day or two, but she left.'

'Left? What was wrong with her?'

'She … wasn't quite suitable, ma'am. But there are two more coming from the agency this afternoon.'

'Blimey!' Louisa said. 'I can't turn my back without … well, I'll pick one myself, this time.'

She bustled off. The three looked at one another, mutually relieved.

'Well done,' the major said softly, and they dispersed.

# CHAPTER SIX

Merriman pushed open the door of Louisa's parlour and entered. He carried a tray on which were a decanter of dry sherry and two glasses. The fire was burning brightly in the little grate. It was cold outside — a cold early autumn morning in 1907.

Louisa was at her desk, making up a bill from a pile of service dockets beside her, watched unseeingly by the framed photographs of two men. Lord Haslemere's was signed with his cheerful scrawl, *Louisa, with Fondest Regards, Charlie.* King Edward the Seventh's was tactfully unsigned.

'Fourteen pounds, plus three pounds eight…' she muttered aloud before looking up. 'Oh, stick it over there,' she told Merriman with a vague gesture. 'I'm expecting my lawyer, Sir Michael Manning. Tell Starr to show him straight in.'

'Yes, madam,' he said, setting the tray down on a small table.

'I'm making up Mr Buckhurst's bill,' she said. 'There's eight bottles of claret down to him, but you've only charged for six.'

'That's right, ma'am. He returned two. He said one was corked and the other was not what he had ordered.'

'Did he? You startin' to slip, Merriman?'

'Certainly not, madam. It was a very good year. He said I'd transferred a label from an empty bottle of good claret on to one of an inferior vintage.'

'He what? And just who does Mr Nigel bleedin' Buckhurst think he is?'

'Other members of the staff have opinions about that.'

'I see. Well, you can take his bill up to him and the sooner he's off these premises for good, the better.'

He took the bill and went. Louisa, flushed with irritation, looked at Charlie's picture and said, 'There's not enough like you about any more, love.'

There was a knock at her door. The major entered. 'Sir Michael Manning, madam,' he said.

Manning came in, wearing a heavy overcoat and carrying his top hat and cane. He was middle-aged, alert and distinguished-looking: the archetypal prosperous solicitor.

'My apologies for being late, Louisa,' he said. 'Some business in Chancery took longer than I expected.'

'That's all right. Nice of you to pop round. Oh, Major, say to Starr that we're not to be disturbed. Not for any reason.'

'Of course, of course," said the major, and went out.

Sir Michael removed his coat, accepted some sherry, and after a brief exchange about the weather asked, 'Now, what's all this about? Your note had a tone of urgency and alarm.'

Louisa found a letter on her desk and passed it to him. 'I got this yesterday from Firbank, Bricelow and Firbank. They're solicitors for the people who lease the Bentinck to me. I can't make head nor tail of it.'

He scanned it quickly, then said, 'It's quite simple, really. They want to renegotiate the lease.'

'It doesn't say that. I could have understood that.'

He smiled. 'Solicitors frequently avoid saying what they mean. That is why, so often, another has to be engaged to translate. The arrangement allows us to live in modest comfort.'

'Huh! Trust you lot to have it all nicely fixed up among yourselves. Are you sure that's what they're after, though?'

'Reading between the lines, I sense that, having granted you a long lease on a decrepit hotel which has now become prosperous, they feel they ought to be getting more ground rent.'

'Well, they can feel what they like. It's my blood and sweat's made the Bentinck what it is. And the lease still has fifty years to run.'

'Fifty-three, to be precise — if you don't break it.' He tapped the letter. 'There's just the slightest suggestion here that you may have done so.'

'How?'

'By allowing gaming parties to run until all hours of the morning. And doubtless they have in mind other things they choose not to commit to paper.'

Louisa knew perfectly well what Sir Michael meant. It was universally known in raffish society that she willingly turned a blind eye to what she termed 'respectable goings-on' in the rooms of solitary gentlemen. 'Respectable', that was, according to her own judgment.

'If they're sayin' I allow street girls to use the place, they're bloody liars,' she said.

The lawyer shook his head. 'They're not saying that. The letter simply refers to that stipulation in the lease which requires that "the aforementioned premises shall be used only and solely for the purposes specified, and not for any purpose which may be deemed to be of an illegal, immoral or otherwise disreputable nature".'

'Bloomin' cheek! What's it got to do with them, so long as I pay the ground rent regular? I can't tell my guests to sing hymns after supper and pack them off to bed at nine prompt.'

'Exactly. I've no doubt that if you agreed to pay more they would be willing to delete the clause under a new agreement.

However, the first move is to find out if they're merely trying it on. There really is no ground for suggesting that the Bentinck could be held in public disrepute. I shall write to these people, informing them, in terms of the utmost legal courtesy, that we don't think their gambit will stand up.'

'Oh, thanks dear,' Louisa said, pouring him another sherry. 'That's taken a real weight off —'

She was interrupted by a commotion outside the door; men's voices were upraised. She heard one demanding, 'Will you get out of the way?' and the major replying, 'I'm sorry, sir — Mrs Trotter gave strict instructions…'

'Excuse me,' Louisa said to Sir Michael and went quickly out, closing the door behind her. She found the major literally barring her doorway against Mr Nigel Buckhurst, who was holding, she noted, her bill. He was in his twenties, dressed in a dandified style, and very red in the face. Merriman hovered uncertainly in the background.

'Thank you, Major,' Louisa said quietly. 'What seems to be the trouble, Mr Buckhurst?'

He sneered. 'Where would you like me to begin? Perhaps with the dilatory and discourteous service of the doddering pensioners you employ? Or the apparent inability of the kitchen staff to supply a simple snack without two hours' notice?'

'It had gone midnight, sir,' Merriman intervened. 'I explained that the kitchen staff had gone to bed, then did my best for you myself.'

'That'll do, Merriman,' Louisa said, still quietly. 'The gentleman hasn't finished.'

'Not by a long chalk. I haven't even started on the general surliness and impertinence of the hall porter, who took ten minutes to fetch me an evening paper, and did it with damned ill grace.'

Merriman was not to be silenced. 'He had four suitcases and a cabin trunk to bring down on the way,' he told Louisa.

Still looking at Buckhurst and keeping ominously calm, Louisa suggested, 'You haven't complained, about your room yet. Must've been something wrong with that.'

'As it happens, yes. I quite clearly asked to be moved to a larger one. The suite on the second floor has been vacant since I arrived. It would have suited me excellently.'

'It's permanently reserved for … a regular patron.'

'Huh! I'm surprised such a creature exists, or that anyone should want to stay here twice.'

Louisa's face reddened now. She snapped back, 'And I'm surprised you've stayed as long as you have. If you'll just settle your bill…'

'I have no intention of paying such an exorbitant sum for such inadequate service.' He held the bill up and ripped it savagely in two.

Starr, coming down the stairs with his luggage, was just in time to see it happen. He paused to hear Mrs Trotter tell the irate guest, whose back he, too, was looking forward to seeing, 'Very well. Since you've torn it in half, I'll only charge you half. Hand over ten pounds twelve shillings and fourpence — *then clear off my premises!*'

Her control had gone now, and the last words were shouted. When Louisa lost her temper she was a daunting spectacle; but Buckhurst didn't quail. He said triumphantly, 'Now, there's an admission that you deliberately tried to overcharge me. Well, you won't get a penny now. That's the price for cheating your guests.'

'Starr,' Louisa ordered the porter, 'get them bags back upstairs. Lock 'em in Mr Buckhurst's room and see that they stay there till he settles his bill — in full.'

Starr turned about and set off back up the stairs. Buckhurst was after him with a bound. Fred, who had been lying obediently in his basket behind the desk, flew out, barking furiously, and went for the man's ankles. And from the dispense, which led off the hall, appeared a police constable, putting on his helmet as he came. He was one of the men on the local beat, and it was his custom, like the rest of them, to pop into the Bentinck on a cold morning for a cup of something warm in the dispense and a chat with Starr or Merriman, his hosts there.

Sir Michael Manning came out, a few seconds later, from Louisa's room, to witness the extraordinary sight of men and pieces of luggage rolling entangled down the staircase. His startled gaze caught the gleam of uniform buttons, and a policeman's helmet rolled unevenly to rest at his feet. Automatically, his mind began to revise the text of the letter he had already envisaged writing to the Bentinck's leaseholders, assuring them primly of the place's respectability.

In a Fleet Street public house, The Vineyard, two young reporters on rival newspapers were enjoying a friendly drink. One of them, whose name was Nelson, of the *Daily Mirror,* was congratulating the other, David Culliford, of the *Morning Banner,* on the prominent by-line his editor had given him on a sensational exposé of life in an East End slum. Culliford, an adventurous and slightly raffish man, had earned his reward the hard way, living in the slum for ten days to gather the sordid material for his article.

'Praise from the competition is especially welcome,' he thanked his friend. 'Millie — two more scotches, please.'

'Just a small one for me,' Nelson said. 'I've got to get back to the office.'

'Harmsworth riding you hard, is he?'

'Not especially. I want to write up a nice little piece I picked up at Bow Street this morning. A Mr Nigel Buckhurst was fined for causing a disturbance at the Bentinck Hotel — injuring the hall porter and assaulting a policeman.'

'That's pretty small beer for the *Mirror,* isn't it?'

'Amusing, though. The woman who runs the Bentinck, Louisa Trotter — you must have heard of her — she was as good as a music-hall turn in court. Even brought a smile to the beak's thin lips. A real character.' He grinned mischievously at Culliford. 'And, of course, there's the added spicy little detail that the accused is your publisher's nephew.'

Culliford's eyebrows rose. If he knew anything about Gerald Bulstrode, principal proprietor of the *Morning Banner,* the tactless Nigel Buckhurst would receive a harder time out of court than in it.

He did. His re-trial took place next day in the office of the *Banner*'s editor, Gordon Lawrie, a cynical Scot in his late forties. Lawrie was not present, though. He had diplomatically removed himself when Nigel Buckhurst had entered, sent for by Bulstrode, who was waiting for him there. Bulstrode's name fitted him well. His pomposity and overbearing manner were his most obvious characteristics. He was in his sixties, grey-haired and frock-coated. On this occasion he was carrying a copy of the *Daily Mirror,* with Nelson's near-hilarious account of the court case angrily ringed in red ink.

Bulstrode bellowed true to form, leaving his nephew little chance to defend himself. There was no defence to offer, anyway. He had sent the policeman sprawling down the stairs, losing his helmet and his dignity. He had sprained Starr's ankle for him, wrestling for possession of his luggage. And he had used disgraceful language. The magistrate had fined him and delivered a swingeing rebuke.

When he had finished finding Buckhurst guilty on the additional charges of humiliating his mother, Bulstrode's sister, and getting the family name into disreputable print, Bulstrode dismissed his nephew without troubling to listen to an apology, and sent for the editor, who came in looking a trifle apprehensive himself. To his relief, Bulstrode smiled and threw the rival newspaper into a waste-paper basket.

'Does 'em good to get a dressing-down occasionally,' he said. 'No more than youthful peccadillo, I expect.' He paused for a moment, then asked, 'Tell me, what do you know of this place in Duke Street?'

Lawrie answered, 'The Bentinck? Not much. I attended a private dinner party there once, about a year ago.'

Bulstrode frowned. 'You surprise me, Lawrie. It hardly sounds the sort of place I'd expect you to frequent. Reading between the lines of that piece, it seems distinctly *demi-mondaine* — little better than a common house of assignation, patronised by all the riff-raff. If I'd known that young man was staying there at all I'd have ordered him out.'

Lawrie said, 'I think, sir, Mr Buckhurst's lawyer painted it in the worst possible colours. My one experience gave me the impression of a well-run establishment. The meal was excellent.'

'Hm! That's not the impression anyone will get from that piece in the *Mirror*. No smoke without fire, I believe. This woman who runs the place —'

'Louisa Trotter.'

'Know anything about her?'

'Eccentric. A real character. But a great cook. I'm afraid she's no time for journalists, though. She told me so to my face when we were introduced. That's her way.'

Bulstrode was looking thoughtful now. 'Might her dislike arise from fear, do you think?'

Lawrie risked a smile. 'I don't imagine she's afraid of anything, that one. What should she fear, sir?'

But his employer was not smiling. 'The integrity and purpose, the proper inquisitiveness of the press, Lawrie. Its capacity for exposing matters which others would prefer concealed. Now, as you are aware, Lawrie, it is my stated position not to interfere with the editorial policy of this newspaper. That is your province. You take the decisions and accept the responsibility. Nevertheless, I reserve the right to make an occasional suggestion to you — and I have such a suggestion to make now.'

Later that morning the editor sent for his promising young feature writer, David Culliford. He had ascertained, in the meantime, that, as he had deduced and hoped, the porter at the Bentinck was temporarily incapacitated with his sprained ankle and the hotel was advertising for a stand-in. Passing on their employer's instructions, Lawrie told the young man to hurry round there and try to get the job. The story of the Bentinck from the inside might make as telling a piece as the slums exposé, and would do its writer much good in the proprietor's eyes.

'Revenge for his nephew's treatment?' Culliford ventured to suggest. The editor shook his head.

'Nothing so trivial as that. Our principal proprietor has a very genuine nose for what sells newspapers. No newspaper ever lost circulation by catering for the prejudices of its readers. Our readers, I don't need to tell you, are the new literates; the working people of this land, now beginning to flex their political muscles. The *Banner* will assist in that exercise, and with twenty-two Labour Party members elected last year there is clearly a horse worth riding.'

'Ah, I see.'

'You'll also be aware that our principal proprietor has certain preoccupations of his own at the moment. Harmsworth's elevation to the peerage has given rise to certain hopes. The proprietor and guiding spirit of a crusading newspaper, dedicated to exposing the injustice of our society, revealing without mercy the moral cancer rotting the fabric of this, that and the other…' The editor gave his cynical smile. 'Such a man must surely find his reward in the Honours List. Do you follow me?'

'Perfectly, sir,' Culliford grinned. 'I'll get round there straight away. Oh, I'd better get a reference first. I know just the place where they'll give me one.'

He hurried round to The Vineyard, bought the landlord and himself a drink, and explained what he wanted. The landlord grinned, gave him a drink in return, and scribbled something on a sheet of notepaper bearing the pub's name.

A quarter of an hour after that, Culliford, calling himself Jenkins and using a slightly roughened version of his natural speaking voice, presented this testimonial to Starr at the desk of the Bentinck. Starr read it, asked a question or two, then, limping painfully, took it in to Louisa, leaving the young man patting Fred's head.

'Very civil and neat about his person,' Starr told Louisa. 'Miles beyond that other chap who tried.'

'What does Fred make of him?'

'Took to him at once, ma'am. Wagged his tail.'

'Sounds promising, then. Wheel him in.'

Louisa was impressed, too. Hall porters were seldom given to being young, healthy, neat and deferential all at the same time. And the landlord of The Vineyard, it seemed, couldn't praise him too highly.

'Why'd you leave there?' she asked.

'To better myself, ma'am. I didn't want to stay a potman all my life. I thought I'd like to make my way in the hotel trade — and this seemed a golden chance to get a bit of experience in the very place to learn.'

'Well,' she said, successfully flattered, 'I can't keep you long. Only till Starr's leg's better. Say a week, guaranteed? It'd be long hours and you'd have to turn your hand to anything that comes up — running errands, helping in the kitchen, seeing the guests' shoes get polished. And I can't pay all that much for a temporary.'

'That's doesn't matter, madam. I'm only too grateful for the chance.'

'Righto. Then you can take it.'

'Thank you very much, madam.'

Approved of by the formidable Mrs Trotter and the infallible Fred, Culliford had achieved his object with perfect ease. He proceeded to make himself as useful as possible from the start, going so far as to volunteer for tasks such as carrying trays for Merriman and saving the disabled Starr the trouble of hobbling out to call cabs for guests. This naturally made a good impression all round — though not quite all round.

Major Smith-Barton, DSO, had been in the Army long enough to know that no man but a fool or a scrounger ever volunteered for anything. This young man was clearly no fool; in fact, in the first conversational exchange between him and the major, he showed himself to be far above the level of intelligence of potmen or temporary hall porters, and much better spoken. Even allowing for the fact that he averred he had merely been starting from the bottom and had much higher ambitions, there was something about him which told the major's instincts that he was not 'quite right'. He said nothing, but his manner towards 'Jenkins' was noticeably cool and cautious.

One evening the new man was working in the hall, vigorously polishing some brasswork which gleamed already, when he heard the major tell Starr at the desk, 'Oh, by the way, young Mr Forbes-Maltby is expecting a guest for supper tonight. You're to show her straight up to his rooms.'

'I'll do that for you, Mr Starr,' Culliford said. 'Save your leg. What name will she give, Major?'

'Any name she fancies,' Starr grinned, and winked. 'It won't be her real one.'

'Anyway, it's none of your business,' the major snapped at the temporary porter. 'I was speaking to Starr.' He marched away, showing disapproval in the way he moved.

'I dunno,' Culliford said to Starr. 'He's took a dislike to me. Been snapping at me since the day I arrived. What've I done?'

'Nothing,' Starr consoled him. 'He can be a funny old cove at times. Ask Fred. He'll tell you.'

'Thanks, Mr Starr,' said the young man. Resuming his polishing, he said casually, 'I thought Mrs Trotter was strict about letting the street girls in.'

'She is. But them's tarts. This one's a lady.' Starr winked at his assistant. 'Just doesn't want to get her husband upset.'

A couple of evenings later, Culliford knocked on Louisa's door and went in to get her coal scuttle for refilling. She wasn't there. Keeping his ears pricked sharply, he went quickly to her desk and glanced over its contents. She had left a letter on her pad, not quite completed. Culliford read it with the swiftness of practice. He noticed the two photographs, one of them affectionately inscribed. He seemed to recognise the face, but couldn't immediately put a name to it. Not daring to risk being any longer, he got the scuttle and went out.

The major, in his usual seat near the hall window, thought casually that it had taken a long time just to fetch a coal scuttle. He resolved that when this strange young fellow went back in with it he would make a point of chancing to go in himself. He was saved the trouble, though: Louisa returned at that moment, and when her temporary porter brought back the full scuttle she was addressing an envelope and placing her finished letter into it.

She gave him a friendly smile. 'Not had an evening off, have you?' she said.

'Oh, that's all right, Mrs Trotter. Only too willing.'

'Look, things are as quiet as the grave,' she said. 'The major's around, if anything crops up.' She stamped the envelope and handed it to him. 'Just drop that in the post for me, there's a dear, and the rest of the evening's your own.'

'Thanks, madam,' he said. 'If I get a move on I might just be in time for the last showing at the Bioscope.'

He hurried out. The major watched him go, disapproving of porters who read the addresses on letters they were given to post. But now David Culliford knew whose the second portrait was. The name had come back to him, for there it was on the envelope, addressed to Lord Haslemere, Bishopsleigh, Yorkshire.

The next morning Louisa was arranging a vase of flowers in her parlour. She cared little about flowers herself, but thought they looked proper to any visitors. Her temporary porter came in, aproned, to say, 'Excuse me, Mrs Trotter. Mr Merriman says to tell you that the new lot from the wine merchant is in the bins now. He's waiting in the cellar to check over the stock list when you're ready.'

'Be down in a minute,' she replied. 'Enjoy the Bioscope last night?'

He hesitated. 'I … didn't go. Well, to tell the truth, there's a young lady serves behind the bar in the place I used to work…'

'Oh, yes?'

'I went along to see if she fancied going with me — it was her night off — but we got talking instead. Serious. In the end I … well, I popped the question.'

'That was quick, wasn't it?'

'Well, I didn't say anything to you before, madam, but I've been offered a situation up north. Nice little pub for a married couple. I've got to take it up by next Wednesday at the latest, so I had to make up my mind and speak to Millie. She said yes.'

'Well, congratulations, I suppose. Sounds like a good beginning.'

'I think so, Mrs Trotter. I was going to ask you today if you could see your way to letting me go? I really ought to go up straight away and make arrangements.'

Louisa nodded. 'Starr's just about mended. Between you and me, I reckon he's been putting it on a bit, these last couple of days. Glad of a rest. You'd have had to go on Friday, anyway. Tell you what, I'll make up your wages to Friday for you and you leave as soon as you like.'

'That's very kind of you, Mrs Trotter,' he said. Although he was a journalist, and ambitious, he was not entirely thick-skinned. He felt even worse when she added, 'And I'll pop a little extra in the envelope as a wedding present.' She refused to let him dissuade her.

That lunchtime he was back in The Vineyard, talking to Millie. Nothing was said of matrimony or of pubs in the north, though. She was perfectly happily married already.

# CHAPTER SEVEN

A week after that found Louisa re-reading, with mounting horror and fury, a long and prominent article in the *Morning Banner*, illustrated with a photograph of the exterior of her hotel. Major Smith-Barton and Starr, who had brought the newspaper in to her, stood uncomfortably by.

*In Duke Street, that discreet and fashionable thoroughfare, is to be found the discreet and fashionable Bentinck Hotel. Discretion is its stock in trade and the proprietress of this very private hotel, Mrs Louisa Trotter, guards its clients and their activities from the ever-curious gaze of the outside world with the zeal of a tigress protecting her cubs.*

*Here, in this temple of wealth and privilege, the rich may disport themselves, secure in the knowledge that no prying eyes will disapprove their indulgences, certain that their indiscretions will go no further than its elegant apartments. Here, they may game from sunset to sunrise, if they wish, or meet with the ladies of their choice in amorous dalliance…*

'Sounds like I'm runnin' a bleedin' whorehouse!' Louisa exploded at last. 'Where the 'ell did they get this stuff from? Who's been staying here pretending to be who they wasn't, and then goin' off writing this muck?'

'It's by one David Culliford,' the major pointed out. 'I can assure you, madam, we've had no journalists here incognito.'

'Well, then, who's been openin' their mouths outside?'

'Your staff are completely loyal to you, Mrs Trotter.'

'Yeh … well, whoever it is knows too much. Even at first glance I can see that he's just changed a name or two, but it's obvious who he means. Coming on top of that court business, this is the last straw.' She jumped up. 'I'm goin' down to the *Banner* now and have it out with that editor. And let 'em try to stop me.'

Of course, they did try to stop her, all the way up from the *Banner*'s foyer to the editor's room; but Louisa Trotter, in determined motion, was an irresistible force. She stormed into the astonished Lawrie's presence, flourishing the by now crumpled copy of his newspaper.

'Do you run this scandal sheet?' she demanded, having run him to earth by dashing about looking for a door labelled EDITOR. 'Half a mo',' she paused to say, as he got to his feet. 'I've met you before.'

He had sensed from the moment he had read David Culliford's copy that there would be trouble coming sooner or later, and here it was, in person. He smiled nervously. 'Yes, I'm the editor, Mrs Trotter. Gordon Lawrie. I had the pleasure of meeting you about a year ago.'

'Well, it won't be a pleasure meeting me again. What do you mean by printing all these lies about my hotel?'

He answered carefully, 'I am confident that we have printed only the truth.'

'Don't tell me what's true and what isn't. No David Culliford's ever been inside its walls.'

'The journalist in question is noted for the accuracy of his reporting, madam. He has based the article on extensive enquiries, following your recent case in court.'

'Has he, indeed? Well, just you get him in here and I'll give him some real home truths.'

The editor shook his head firmly. 'Out of the question, Mrs Trotter. Quite apart from the fact that such a thing is never done, Mr Culliford is not in the building at present.'

Louisa looked round for a chair and went to sit in it. 'Then I'll wait till he comes back,' she declared. 'I shan't budge until I see him. And it's no use thinking of having me carried out kicking and screaming.'

Lawrie was eyeing her speculatively. He puzzled her by saying slowly, 'No. Not without illustrations.' He strode from his room and a few minutes later came back with a photographer, who proceeded to set up his tripod camera and prepare his flash pan.

The door opened again and Bulstrode came in, carrying a proof. He stared about in surprise at the photographer, the defiantly seated woman, and the editor, also seated, looking on with what seemed to be grim amusement.

'A photographic session, Mr Bulstrode,' Lawrie explained. 'May I introduce Mrs Louisa Trotter, of the Bentinck Hotel? Mr Bulstrode, our proprietor.'

'Madam,' Bulstrode greeted her, with an automatic little bow.

Lawrie continued, 'Mrs Trotter declines to leave my office until she has spoken to Culliford. I have, of course, declined to permit the interview.'

'Quite correct, I'm afraid, Mrs Trotter. But … why the photograph, Lawrie?'

'It will enhance the page on which our further article on the Bentinck is printed. Indeed, Mrs Trotter has kindly offered our readers the spectacle of her being carried struggling from the room by the two commissionaires I was just about to summon.'

Bulstrode slowly broke into a broad smile. 'An excellent notion! I will write the caption for it myself.'

'You're not taking my bleedin' picture,' Louisa said, beaten. She got up. 'You call yourselves men?'

With all the dignity she could muster she swept out, to a bow, mocking this time, from Bulstrode. She heard their laughter behind her. At the pitch of her humiliated fury, she turned the corner of the passage — and walked straight into David Culliford.

There was just one moment's pause for mutual recognition. Then Louisa swung her hand all the way up from her side and gave him a cracking slap across one cheek, before marching on without speaking a word.

Back at the Bentinck she paraded the major, Starr and Merriman and told them what she had found out. The major started to speak, but she silenced him.

'Not one word. Not one bloody word!' She turned on Starr. 'As for reckonin' to be a judge of character… You oughter have that bloody mongrel of yours put down, too.'

She was calmer but unrepentant that evening when she entertained Sir Michael Manning privately to dinner. The interview was at his urgent request.

'My dear Louisa,' he told her, 'the impulse was understandable, but to call round to see them — even worse to assault one of them physically — a grave mistake. Still, I suppose it can be presented as an instance of innocence outraged. It may not prejudice our case too badly.'

'Case? What case?'

He looked surprised. 'You can't possibly let matters rest, don't you see? The damage done by that article could be enormous. You must proceed against this newspaper for libel.'

'Oh, no! Please, no lawyers. No letters.'

'It need never reach court. A printed apology, a retraction, and an agreed sum of money…'

'D'you think they'd wear it?'

'Since you appear to have left the editor and the proprietor uninjured, it is just possible. But if they decline, you must be prepared to go all the way against them.'

She shrugged. 'I suppose I'll lose a bit of custom. Maybe attract some I don't want. But the Bentinck's reputation will recover. No, I'd sooner forget the whole thing.'

The lawyer asked uncomfortably, 'Louisa, answer me very carefully. Is there any substance in Culliford's article?'

Her eyes flashed, but she had to say, 'Well … it's true and it isn't. It's more the way he's written it. That bit that refers to young Forbes-Maltby. It reads like the girl's some tart.'

'We could produce Mr Forbes-Maltby to refute that.'

'God, no! There'd be a divorce. Anyway, I told you, I'm not going near a court.'

'I'm afraid you have no alternative,' he had to tell her at last. 'A note of hand was delivered to me today, requesting me to call round for a word with Firbank, Bricelow and Firbank. I spoke to the senior partner. It's no longer a simple matter of trying to increase the ground rent. The lessors wish to see the lease terminated as soon as possible. They object to having their premises used as … well, in their own words, as a house of ill-fame.'

'But … they can't do that, can they? Not just because some gossip-monger…'

'I'm afraid that if we allow this report to go unchallenged it will be taken as an admission that there is truth in the allegation,' he warned her emphatically.

Louisa could only sigh deeply and agree to let him set it all in motion.

Two days later, Gordon Lawrie, editor of the *Morning Banner,* read out to his chief proprietor a letter which had just come by hand.

'…*this being so, unless a full and agreed retraction is published and given equal prominence, and unless compensation is offered for the damage sustained by my client, she will have no alternative but to seek a writ for libel against your newspaper and all those persons connected with the matter. I remain, et cetera … Sir Michael Manning.*'

The editor said anxiously, 'Manning. The lady can afford the best.'

'But we can afford better,' Bulstrode comforted him. 'So long as you can assure the Board that young Culliford's piece was accurate.'

'As I told Mrs Trotter, I believe we printed the truth.'

'In the public interest. Quite so. Then be assured that I shall stand behind you.'

With Scottish candour, Lawrie told his employer, 'Since the suggestion for the article was your own, I should have thought that beside me would be a more appropriate position.'

'Indeed, indeed,' Bulstrode said smoothly. 'Yes, I recall having made several suggestions, so I can hardly quarrel with the fact that you found one worthy of attention. The manner of its execution is, of course, your responsibility — and you are aware of my feelings on the subject of editorial responsibility.'

It was a constantly recurring theme of his, always reiterated at great length. His editor regarded him suspiciously.

'Am I to understand, Mr Bulstrode, that this threatened libel action is going to be solely my concern?'

'And Culliford's, of course. You will appreciate that I myself can't become involved. Wrong assumptions might be made about why the piece was published.'

'Your nephew?'

Bulstrode smiled. 'You take my point exactly.'

When he had gone, Lawrie made urgent enquiries for David Culliford. The consensus of opinion was that at this time of day — it was lunchtime — he would almost certainly be in The Vineyard. Lawrie was not a drinking man and felt a strong aversion to Fleet Street's pubs. Too much talent, too much potentially good writing had evaporated in their smoke and fumes, in his opinion. Nevertheless, today he went at once to The Vineyard and was relieved to find Culliford as soon as he entered. He recognised the surprise on his writer's face.

'Yes, yes. The taverns of this street have been the ruination of many good journalists, and not a few bad ones,' he said. 'But I wish to talk to you urgently, where our conversation can be informal and unofficial. I intend, if need be, to deny that it ever took place.' To this portentous opening he added, 'You may purchase for me a glass of seltzer or something equally innocuous, and join me in the corner there.'

When David came back with the soda water and another whisky for himself — a neat one, so that it might appear small to his disapproving editor — Lawrie looked around, then asked in a low tone, 'This Bentinck business. You are quite certain of the facts?'

'Of course, sir. I've full notes of who went there during my time, and for what purpose — plus a lot of entries copied from the register.'

Lawrie showed little relief. He explained, 'When you say, "for what purpose", have you any proof that those purposes were carried out?'

'Well, no. I couldn't go that far.'

'So it can only be speculation — in which case a libel action might well succeed. I don't mind admitting I've feared this all along.'

'But we haven't been threatened, have we?'

'This morning. Retract or we sue, they're saying.'

'You're not going to print a retraction, are you … sir?' Culliford asked, suddenly fearful for his reputation in the Street.

'Not at all. Mr Bulstrode has set his face firmly against it. Therefore, we must persuade Mrs Trotter to drop the action or —' he looked round again before continuing — 'destroy her character to such an extent that the action will fail. A woman of that sort has a past, and you would do well to set straight about discovering what that past is.'

As he had done several times while writing his article and since, Culliford thought unhappily of Louisa's generous gesture towards the supposed temporary hall porter, and felt again a sense of having betrayed her. 'I … doubt if there's much to find out,' he answered.

'You must have overheard servants' gossip.'

'Nothing worth remembering.'

The editor said, 'I detect a certain lack of enthusiasm.'

'Well … why go on persecuting her, sir?'

'To prevent her from prosecuting us, Culliford. You and me, as author and editor respectively. Of course, the *Banner* will be sued with us, as printer and publisher. But don't let it escape your notice that we are mere individuals, while it is an organisation.'

'You mean … they wouldn't stand by us?'

'They'd have to — but only up to a point. I've already had some intimation of where that point might be. It could have a calamitous effect on both our careers. Now, where do we start with Louisa Trotter?'

Culliford took a pull at his whisky and said, 'I'll need to go to New Yarmouth.'

Two evenings later he was back in The Vineyard, this time in the more familiar company of Nelson from the *Mirror*.

'Thought you'd signed the pledge, or something,' the latter said, paying for their drinks. 'Thought he'd deserted us, didn't we, Millie?'

'Yes, duckie. By the way, Mr Culliford, there's been a man asking for you. An oldish codger. Been in several times, lunchtime and evenings.'

'Did he give you a message, or his name?'

'No. Just kept asking… Oh! Here 'e comes now.'

Culliford turned to the door and was startled to see Major Smith-Barton advancing towards him. He hurriedly excused himself from Nelson and went to intercept the older man.

'Evening, Major,' he said as cheerfully as he could. 'Can I get you a drink?'

The major's expression of affront and contempt answered him. 'You're a rogue and a scoundrel,' he said. 'If I were a younger man, I'd thrash you.'

Culliford was stung to retort, 'Tied to the wheel of a gun carriage, I suppose?' But he regretted the insult and looked sheepish.

Major Smith-Barton pulled a piece of paper from his breast pocket. Culliford recognised it as the testimonial he had got the landlord of this pub to write for him as 'Jenkins'.

'If you're wondering how I found you, it was through this,' the major said. 'I suspected you from the start. I have come to appeal to any decent feelings you might have left. You have injured a fine woman. Caused her great distress. She hasn't been sleeping for nights. Now, it seems, she's going to lose her hotel.'

This really startled the younger man. 'Mrs Trotter's going to lose the Bentinck!'

111

'Something to do with the lease, don't you know? And all because of your lying innuendos.'

There was no note of triumph in Culliford's response to this. He said unhappily, 'I'm afraid there's worse still to come, Major. I've just returned from New Yarmouth. I got an interview there with Mr Trotter. Mr Augustus Trotter.'

'That does it, then,' Louisa groaned when the major reported this to her, half an hour later. 'The fat's in the fire, and no mistake. One bottle of brandy and my dear husband'll talk for a week — and throw in a song for good measure.'

Although she spoke flippantly, she was deeply worried and disturbed. Once more, it seemed that all she had built up was collapsing on top of her. She sensed that even her resilient spirit might be crushed incurably this time.

The major went on, 'He declined to reveal what Mr Trotter told him. I thought he might tell you, though. I formed the impression that he was quite anxious to come and see you, so I, er, prevailed upon him to return with me, don't you know?'

'Culliford's *here*?'

'In the hall. And Starr's having to keep a tight hold on his dog's collar — though I fancy he'd sooner let him loose.'

'Better show him in, then.'

'Would you like me to stay, too?'

'No thanks. I can manage Master bloody Culliford on me own.'

The journalist was duly ushered in and the door closed. Louisa had seated herself magisterially. She kept him standing.

'I suppose you're proud and pleased with yourself?' she said icily.

'Pride doesn't come into it, Mrs Trotter. I do my job as best I can, and I think it's worth doing.'

'Call it a job? There's girls on the street outside got jobs more worth doing. Some job, worming your way in here with lies and then printing more lies in your rotten newspaper.'

'I reported what I saw and heard,' he answered resolutely.

'What you wanted to see, you mean.'

'Mrs Trotter, a few weeks ago I wrote about what it was like to live in an East End slum — the squalor, the hunger, the hopelessness. The sheer brutality of the fight to survive. Then I come to a place like this. A place where the worst tragedy that can happen is a soufflé going flat.'

'Oh, Gawd, where've I heard all this before? Anyway, what's wrong with helping other people have a bit of fun and pleasure?'

'Possibly the girls on the street might give the same answer.'

Instinctively he took a step backwards as Louisa's eyes flared and she looked wildly around. One of the many things her husband had told him under the influence of brandy was of the last time he had seen his wife, as he and his sister had retreated before her hail of bottles.

'I'm sorry, Mrs Trotter,' he said earnestly. 'Don't hit me again, please. We have an important matter to discuss.'

'Yes. What Gus told you.'

'He was … very forthcoming.'

'You mean he was drunk.'

'Drunk and bitter, Mrs Trotter. He seems to think he's been treated very badly. But he'll be sober enough in the witness box, if it comes to it, and I'm afraid what he has to say won't do your reputation any good. Mrs Trotter, if you drop this action, I've good reason to believe my employers are prepared to forget the whole matter.'

'If I drop this action, I'll lose the lease on my hotel. Look, couldn't you say you made a mistake — that you'd got it all wrong? I wouldn't want damages. If you just printed that…'

'Then the *Banner* would be made to look foolish — and I'd lose my job.'

'What about my hotel?' she said, knowing that she had lost the initiative.

Culliford didn't like one bit having to apply so relentlessly what he had come to recognise as moral blackmail. He felt sincerely sorry for her. But if she was in a corner, he was in one opposite her. One or the other of them had to lose, and he would fight rather than let it be himself.

'You have a difficult decision to make, Mrs Trotter,' he lectured her. 'When I said that your husband was forthcoming, I meant it. He instanced several things…'

His gaze had left hers. She saw where he was looking — at the photographs of Lord Haslemere and His Majesty the King — and she no longer doubted that her world was about to crash.

For once in her life, Louisa pleaded with someone. She begged him to keep to himself matters which would bring great hurt and grievance to other people. Matters which lay in the past and had no bearing on her conduct of the Bentinck Hotel. Despite his feelings, Culliford was adamant. He left soon afterwards with no concession made, and she immediately penned a note to Sir Michael Manning, instructing him to drop all plans for a libel action.

When he reported back to his office, Culliford went at once to see his editor. Lawrie listened unhappily, then shrugged his shoulders and told him to get on and write the second article. His last hope seemed to be that if Culliford could contrive to

114

let Mrs Trotter see it before it went into print, she might just be shocked into surrender.

'Put it all in,' he instructed. 'The worse it reads, the better; but nothing but fact, though. Either way, we've got to make sure of winning.'

Culliford went away and began to write. As his article grew he realised what a sensational scoop it represented for his paper, and his mind's eye pictured his by-line on it and the congratulatory smiles of his superiors. And then he paused, suddenly remembering something the editor had said to him that morning. He thought for a while, wrestling with his inclinations this way and that. Then he began to write again, this time with a grim smile set almost permanently on his countenance.

When he had finished he took his copy to the editor, and watched with some amusement the appalled expression on his face as he read. Finally Lawrie looked up.

'For God's sake, take it and show her it,' he ordered. 'There'll be repercussions all over the world if this gets into print. She wouldn't dare let us run it.'

But Culliford had a counter-suggestion ready. He put it. Lawrie looked at first startled, then intrigued. At length he nodded agreement.


That evening, with Sir Michael Manning already present, Louisa coolly but politely greeted the *Morning Banner*'s principal proprietor in her parlour. His secretary had telephoned an hour earlier to request the honour of an urgent appointment.

Louisa had had sherry laid out. Bulstrode accepted his glass with a determinedly conciliatory smile.

'Your very good health, Mrs Trotter,' he said, somewhat surprisingly. 'Ah, excellent! To come straight to the point, now.

I have read young Culliford's further article about you. Some of its contents shocked me considerably, but I obtained the boy's assurance that they represent the truth, as obtained from your husband. I have brought the article with me, and if you would care to read it for yourself before I continue…?'

'No, thanks,' Louisa said bitterly. 'I know what it'll be. I don't want to see it spelled out.'

'Exactly. Now, when I myself came to the passages concerning your, ah, conjugal difficulties, I paused to consider the matter very carefully. My heart is not of stone, Mrs Trotter, and I have no wish to drive you to the wall. While your attitude has scarcely been conciliatory…'

'It was your rotten paper that started it!' she burst out.

Sir Michael touched her restrainingly and said, 'Please, Louisa. I think Mr Bulstrode has a proposition to put.'

'I have.' The other man nodded. 'I have never been a man to bear a grudge, and I have certainly no desire to injure an … an innocent child; nor, for that matter, to cause unnecessary distress to its mother. In other words, I have decided that if you are prepared to abandon this ill-advised suit, it is possible that I might be able to meet you halfway.'

The lawyer asked, 'Plainly, Mr Bulstrode — will you print a retraction?'

'I am willing to consider — no more than consider — the possibility that our writer, Mr Culliford, may have overstated certain facts in the original article. I say "may have", Sir Michael. I admit to nothing.'

'Then what form would the retraction take?'

Bulstrode drew himself up and in his most pompous manner replied, 'The *Banner* will not grovel, let that be clear. I have in mind a brief but dignified expression of regret that the wrong impression may have been conveyed. That the *Banner* now accepts that the Bentinck Hotel is an establishment of the utmost respectability. That its proprietress is a lady of impeccable reputation…' Suddenly he could keep up the excessive dignity no longer. He relaxed visibly and smiled at Louisa. 'Oh, you know the sort of thing, Mrs Trotter. We can leave the precise wording to the lawyer johnnies. No offence, Sir Michael.'

'I accept,' Louisa said promptly.

'Now, Louisa, don't be hasty!' Sir Michael cautioned her, but she insisted.

'I accept, I accept, I accept!'

Bulstrode smiled again and told the lawyer, 'Sir Michael, you would appear to have your client's instructions.'

Louisa poured more sherry for them all.


'What do you want?' Starr growled suspiciously that same night when David Culliford presented himself at the reception desk. Fred was growling steadily too.

The journalist held up a copy of the first edition of next morning's *Banner*, which he had snatched straight from the printing press and brought round by cab. 'She'll want to see this,' he answered.

Reluctantly, Starr admitted him to Louisa's parlour. Despite the release of tension she had experienced only a few hours earlier, she was still at her desk, drinking wine, smoking a cigarette, and fiddling distractedly with this piece of paper and that.

'Be careful,' Culliford warned her. 'The ink's still wet.'

'Never mind that,' she said, unheeding, and dirtied her fingers in her haste to read the promised notice of retraction. 'Well,' she said at last, throwing the newspaper into her waste-paper basket, 'it'll do. And now I've seen it, you can push off and rake around for some dirt elsewhere.'

He smiled. 'I am clearing off — well out of harm's way. Tomorrow, as it happens. I've been appointed the *Banner*'s correspondent in New York. Quite a step up.'

'Well, I hope you're seasick all the way.'

'Thank you. It ought to be a relief to know that your secrets are three thousand miles away.'

'It's no thanks to you they're still secrets at all!'

'You'd be surprised,' he said. His steady smile puzzled her. 'You see, I wrote the whole thing in as lurid a manner as the facts would allow. When I ran out of facts I invented some. It made the paper curl.'

'Then I take back what I said about being seasick. I hope you fall off the dock at Southampton.'

'Mr Bulstrode was very impressed. But, of course, he decided not to print it.'

'Shows there's some gentlemen left.'

'Oh, his ambitions run higher than being a gentleman. He's even got his title chosen for the Honours List. So he's not likely to offend the one man who can see that his name doesn't appear in it, is he?'

Louisa stared uncomprehendingly. For once, her quick mind was not up to the pace of what seemed to be going on about her. The young journalist was pausing aggravatingly, leaving the implications to fall into place. Eventually, Louisa said slowly, 'He … said it was for the sake of my … kid. And she's got … nothing to do with … a certain personage.'

Culliford grinned. 'Somehow or other, Mr Bulstrode got the notion that she had.'

She spelled it out frankly. 'The king isn't her father.'

He shrugged. 'Must've been the way I wrote it, then.'

There was a very long silence. Then Louisa said, 'Have a glass of wine before you go.'

'Thanks, Mrs Trotter.'

While she was pouring it he was fishing out his wallet and extracting two pound notes. He placed them on her desk.

'I owe you a couple of quid,' he said. 'Return of unused wedding present.'

# CHAPTER EIGHT

Ascot Week, in June, was always one of Louisa's periods of peak activity. The Bentinck was full of long-reserved people up from the country. There were nightly parties in most of the suites, with much coming and going of guests' guests. On top of it, her services were in hectic demand for outside catering; and there were still the accounts to keep up to date, never Louisa's favourite activity.

On the morning of the day before the end of Ascot, 1908, she sat at her desk desperately adding: '…and 4 is 19, 21, 27, 35, 2 carry 4 … come in,' she said automatically in response to a knock on the door. She didn't raise her head.

'Hello, Louisa,' said a voice from the past which caused her to look up quickly. She smiled in real pleasure to see her old friend Major Sir John Farjeon, former equerry to the king and go-between in his relationship with her.

'Johnnie!' she cried. 'Well, I'm blowed!'

'It's been a long time,' he agreed, pleased too.

'How are you?' she asked. 'I seen you got married. Seems to suit you. Put on a bit of weight, haven't you?'

'That's a secret between me and my tailor.'

'And I seen in the *Gazette* you gave up the equerry lark. Couldn't stand the pace, eh?'

'Not that and marriage. I'm back with the Battalion now. Second-in-Command.'

'Good for you. So what're you doing here?'

'Phillida — my wife — she's, well, a bit raw, but fearfully keen to do things properly. So we took a small house down at

Ascot, just for the week. A small house party — six of us. Should have been ideal, but it's turned out an unmitigated disaster.'

'Guests not get on?'

'That's only one of the problems. The staff we've inherited defy description. And the cooking … Louisa, I was hoping you'd help me take the curse off the whole thing by organising a really good dinner party for tomorrow — the last day?'

'Tomorrow! I've got seven dinners already, never mind about running the hotel.'

'Yes, I imagined you'd be pushed. I wouldn't have asked if … Charlie hadn't said you'd help if you possibly could. He's one of the house guests,' he added, trying to sound casual.

Louisa saw through it. 'And he put you up to it, did he? I might have known. You crafty couple of —'

Major Farjeon interrupted quickly, 'Actually, it all started because the palace has offered me a sturgeon. I've been on the list a long time. It seemed providential for a very special dinner, only the cook we've got couldn't even do sardines on toast. Besides, it's the royal fish, and Charlie rightly pointed out that it needs the queen of cooks to do justice to it.'

Flattery on such lines influenced the snob in Louisa a great deal, as Farjeon and Haslemere were aware. She protested again, but agreed. 'How many will you be?' she asked.

'Ten, all told.'

'How's your cellar down there?'

'Deplorable.'

'Sounds like you ought to ask for your money back. You'll want me to do the wines as well, then?'

'Everything, please, Louisa.'

'How big's this sturgeon? And have I got to have it picked up, or will they send it over?'

'I've no idea,' he said vaguely, vastly relieved to relinquish all responsibility.

'Oh, run along!' she scolded. 'I'll telephone the bloomin' palace myself.'

When he had gone she summoned Major Smith-Barton, her adviser on fine wines. 'What would you serve with sturgeon?' she asked.

'Well, a Rhône, I'd say. The '99 Hermitage, perhaps? Or, of course, the Puligny Montrachet '02, if you really want to spoil 'em, don't you know?'

'That'll do,' she said, writing it down.

'When is this for?'

'Tomorrow. An extra client.'

'But I thought…'

'Yes, I know we're booked right up. But this is an extra-*special* client — a friend of Charlie's. I'll have to ask you to help out, if you can.'

'With pleasure, madam,' the major said. 'And speaking of Charles, I was meaning to ask you how well he knows Desmond Elleston?'

'Why?'

'He owns Vital Spark — the racehorse, don't you know? Well fancied for the Alexandra Plate tomorrow. I've got one sure-fire tip — Bembo, for the Hardwicke Stakes. I was thinking about making Vital Spark the second leg of a double. Wondered whether Charles would have any inside advice?'

Louisa got up. 'I'll give you mine for nothing. Save your money. With your luck, the odds on them both dropping down dead is the only ones you'll double. Do yourself a favour, Major. As far as Ascot goes, you stick to driving the 'bus for me tomorrow.'

They returned to the subject of wines. Eventually, Louisa had her menu complete:

*Consommé*
*Esturgeon Farci*
*Soufflé de Cailles*
*Pièces de Boeuf à la Gelée en Bellevue*
*Asperges en Branches*
*Fraises Natures*
*Le Café*
*Les Petit Fours*

They agreed on the Montrachet with the sturgeon and a '94 claret with the beef. The major also recommended three bottles of Madeira, three of Imperial Tokay, a Quinta de Noval '68 port, and a 15-year-old Exshaw brandy.

All these things were duly assembled the following day and delivery taken of the sturgeon, that mighty fish which, when rarely caught in British waters, automatically becomes the property of the sovereign, to eat or give to some favoured applicant.

As usual when going to cook in a kitchen strange to her, Louisa took no chances with the equipment. Where she had once had to hire one or even two cabs to carry her own, she now had the gleaming hotel 'bus. Into it went the ingredients for the meal, the wines, the condiments even, and all manner of accessories — including, on this occasion, a huge fish kettle. Mrs Cochrane accompanied Louisa, who had to leave behind her kitchen helpers to help Mary run the packed hotel.

'Did you have a word with the couple in Number 7?' Mary asked Louisa through the 'bus window.

'Oh, yes, I almost forgot. You were dead right. They couldn't begin to pay their bill.'

'I knew it all along,' Mary said. 'Told you, I did, ma'am.'

'I know. Should've asked them sooner. But the way he came out with admitting it, I couldn't help but laugh. They've got style, those two, and there's not so much of it about as there was.'

Mary knew her employer's prejudices and methods by now. 'What are you going to do about the money, then?'

'I stuck it on Sir George's bill. Clerical error if he finds out, which he won't. He just pays up.' It was a long-standing custom of Louisa's to rob the rich to pay the poor, so long as the latter amused her, or had her sympathy for some reason or other, or innocently appealed to her eccentric standards.

Mary smiled resignedly and waved as the major engaged the gear and drove the 'bus away down Duke Street.

A pleasant drive took them into Surrey. Eventually the major turned the vehicle in at the gates of what proved to be a large, ugly red-brick Victorian house.

'Ugh!' Louisa ejaculated. 'No wonder they need a decent meal.'

'Nothing much to feast the eyes on, what?' the major agreed, instinctively preparing to drive to the front door. Louisa had to remind him quickly that they were there as servants, not house guests.

'Sorry. One forgets, don't you know?' he said, and took the 'bus round the back.

The back door was opened to them by a 'tweeny' so young-looking that she might have been a child. She was unsmiling and appeared tired beyond her years. A gloomy passageway stretched behind her.

'Who are you?' Louisa asked kindly.

124

'Kath, ma'am.'

'Well, I'm Mrs Trotter. I'm here to do the dinner.'

The unmistakable figure of a butler was approaching, lofty and in late middle age. His manner was civil enough, though, and noticeably worried. He introduced himself as Mr Sterling, and began to apologise at once. 'The kitchen staff's in uproar, Mrs Trotter. When he let the house for the races the master sent the regular staff on holiday, excepting myself and young Kath here. This lot are from an agency, and they've been nothing but trouble from start to finish.'

'Come on,' Louisa said grimly, and marched in, calling over her shoulder to the major and Mrs Cochrane to start unloading.

She made her instinctive way to the kitchen, took one glance round it, and recognised that it was ill-equipped, grubby and untidy. The description might have applied also to the cook, her two assistants and the footman, who were ranged up in stony assembly.

Mr Sterling made introductions. No one moved or smiled.

'What's the matter?' Louisa asked him, in mock surprise. 'All deaf and dumb?'

'We've been insulted, that's what's the matter,' the cook spoke up. 'Bringing you down 'ere. This is my kitchen.'

'Looks like it,' Louisa retorted pointedly. The irony was lost on the woman.

'You touch one thing in here, and we all gives our notice.'

The major and Mrs Cochrane entered with the first load.

'Give in your notice?' Louisa said. 'I can't wait that long. Touch *one* thing, was it? Well, how'll this do, then?' She picked up a large knife and brandished it. 'There. And you'd better get out before I'm tempted to use it on you. I've come here to do a friend an especial favour, and I'm not having it spoiled by a crew like you. So make up your minds — either knuckle down to it as I tell you, or get out.'

With a glance at one another they shuffled silently away.

'Good riddance!' Louisa said loudly after them; but Mrs Cochrane was looking aghast.

'We're going to be ever so short-handed, ma'am,' she pointed out.

'You don't, er, feel her ladyship should have been consulted first?' the butler ventured to suggest.

'She's at the races, isn't she?' Louisa replied. 'Then if we'd stood here arguin' till she got back there wouldn't have been any dinner at all, would there? Now, what other staff have you got?'

'Only outdoor.'

'Visiting valets? Lady's maids?'

'There's Sir John Farjeon's soldier servant, Guardsman Wilson, and Lady Farjeon's maid, Miss Jennett. We've been looking after the others between us.'

'Fetch them in here,' Louisa ordered unhesitatingly.

'It's … most irregular…'

'It's all hands to a sinkin' ship. Don't you see?'

He did, and without further protest went to fetch the other two servants and explain the situation to them. Fortunately, neither objected to helping serve the dinner, though Jennett, a pleasant young woman, rightly pointed out, 'The trouble is, you'll lose us when they're dressing for dinner. Just when you need us most.'

'Can't be in two places at once,' agreed Guardsman Wilson, who hadn't been able to suppress an instinct to snap to attention when introduced to Major Smith-Barton, and kept calling him 'sir', while wondering what on earth this sporty-looking gent could be doing in a kitchen.

Louisa replied, 'We'll all have to be quick on our feet, that's all. Major, you'll have to be acting unpaid dogsbody.'

'With pleasure, Mrs Trotter,' the incredulous Wilson heard him say.

Louisa turned to Kath. 'Going to risk it, love?' she asked, with her warmest smile.

The maid smiled herself, for the first time.

'Good girl. Well, you're kitchen maid, so that's one problem solved. Now, first off, we've all got to clean this kitchen from top to bottom, or we're liable to poison the lot of 'em. Mr Sterling, perhaps you could stretch a point and help the major finish unloading the 'bus?'

The butler was thoroughly into the spirit of it now. He gave a little bow and went to do as she had asked.

For the rest of the morning and all the afternoon they toiled, with only the briefest respite for a snack lunch at staggered intervals. As soon as the sink area had been thoroughly scoured and the preparing table scrubbed, Kath was given the vegetables and told how to prepare them. Her willingness made up for her lack of experience. After a few minutes' supervision, Louisa was confident to leave her to it.

When the old-fashioned range had been de-grimed and degreased, Mrs Cochrane was enabled to start the beef and turn her attention to boning and stuffing the fish. Again, Louisa had to supervise. Mrs Cochrane had never handled sturgeon before. In fact, though everyone worked with a will, it was Louisa who was here, there and everywhere, ordering, advising, supervising, checking, while at the same time performing a myriad tasks of her own.

'Beef?' she demanded of Mrs Cochrane, who opened the oven door for inspection. 'Baste it regular, and turn the pan round in about half an hour.' Louisa turned to Kath. 'Veg?'

The maid displayed the peeled potatoes, waiting in a basin of cold water. Louisa said, 'Keep changing the water until they're actually put on. Makes 'em a better colour. Strawberries, Jennett.' They were ready, in a big dish under a damp cloth. Wilson was also on parade with filled bowls of cream and sugar.

At length, Louisa was able to announce that they had won the battle so far. They were wilting, but she, who had done twice or thrice as much as any of them showed no tiredness, and they copied her example.

'Thank you, one and all,' she said. 'Now there's time for a nice drop of wine before they get back from the races.'

To her surprise, Sterling produced a bottle of champagne at once.

'You're catching on,' she said admiringly.

'The major gave me the hint.'

'Trust him!'

They all laughed and enjoyed a drink together. Sterling and poor Kath both felt, in their different ways, that this was the only happy time they had known all that week.

Much less happy was the newly wed Lady Farjeon, when she returned that evening to find her staff all gone except for Sterling and Kath, and her own and her husband's personal servants laying the dining table. 'Mrs Trotter,' she complained, with the outraged dignity of a young wife who is conscious of her authority but out of her depth in exercising it, 'I find that you haven't been five minutes in the house before half the staff have given notice — simply walked out.'

'You're better off without them,' Louisa said, carrying on with what she was doing in the dining room, though at least having had the tact to shoo away the others who had been assisting her there. 'I know just how you feel, dear, but if I'd had that lot of weary willies under my feet you'd never have got your dinner.'

Lady Farjeon goggled at this roughly and bluntly spoken woman. 'You don't seem to realise. We have a house party.'

'Finish tomorrow, don't you?' Louisa said, straightening spoons.

'I know. But someone has to give them breakfast.'

'Oh, if that's all that's worrying you, I'll see to it. Leave it all so's Kath and Sterling have only to heat it up and serve it.'

'Can … you really…?'

'I'll have it done by the time dinner's been washed up. Now, how d'you like the flowers?'

'They're … lovely.'

'I like to do me own flowers. Seen the menu, have you?'

She shoved one into Lady Farjeon's hand. The latter could only stammer, 'I don't … see how it could be bettered.'

'No, it couldn't. But it's really nice of you to say so, dear. I heard you'd had a bad week, one way and another. We had to try and do something a bit special for you. You've not been married long, have you?'

'N-no.'

'Lovely fellow you got there — Johnnie. I reckon he hasn't done so bad, either.'

'You're an amazing woman, Mrs Trotter,' conceded Lady Farjeon, overwhelmed and disarmed.

'Thanks, dear. Just so long as you have an amazing evening.'

'Oh, I think we shall. I *really* think we shall.'

They laughed together suddenly, and the sound penetrated to the smoking room, where the men were sitting over their pre-dinner drinks. Charles Tyrrell, Lord Haslemere, had insisted on Major Smith-Barton — his father's ex-fag from Eton days — joining them. The only absentee was Lady Farjeon's godfather,

George Ross. Upon entering the house in a foul mood he had gone straight off to his room to bathe.

'Peace reigns supreme in the dining room, it seems,' Farjeon remarked with relief, having raised his head to listen to the two women's laughter.

'But not throughout the household,' Charlie Haslemere breathed into his whisky. 'Look, Johnnie, Phillida's godfather or not, if he makes one more accusation about Vital Spark, I'm warning you there'll be trouble.'

The major, who had pricked up his ears, said, 'Oh, ah, Vital Spark? Second favourite and widely fancied. I almost made him the second leg of a double, don't you know?'

'Count your blessings,' Charlie told him.

'Oh? What, er, happened?'

'He simply faded. Don't understand it.'

'No,' said Sir John Farjeon grimly. 'Nor did Phillida's godfather.'

'Well, he's as rich as Croesus,' Charlie said. 'He can afford to lose a packet.'

'That doesn't mean to say he likes to. It's how he stays rich. He keeps hinting that there was something funny about it,' Farjeon explained to the major, who, despite his equivocal position in Louisa's hotel, was clearly her confidant, and could therefore safely be taken to be an honest man.

'Ah!' was all the major said, though he was looking thoughtful. He got up and screwed his eyeglass into place. 'If you'll excuse me, gentlemen. The second gong will be going soon. Better send your soldier servant up to you, Major Farjeon, sir, hadn't I?'

'Yes,' said Sir John, with a concealed wink at Charlie. 'If you would, sir.'

In the kitchen, Kath watched open-mouthed as Louisa delicately spooned gelatine over the *pièces de boeuf*, transforming what had been a platter of plain garnished sliced beef into a subject worthy of a master of still-life painting. Without realising it she had been holding her breath in wonder. Now she let it all out in one great sigh of relief and admiration.

'It's like a picture!' she declared.'

'That's how it should be,' Louisa nodded, satisfied. 'The first job I ever had, d'you know what the *chef de cuisine* told me there?' She achieved a passable imitation of the accent of her mentor, Monsieur Alex, at Lord Henry Norton's house in Charles Street, Mayfair: '"The most important things, they are, first, ze smell…"' She tapped her nose, in the way she had never forgotten he had done. '"After ze smell, ze taste — ze tongue. And zen — ze *eyes!*"'

Louisa was surprised to see the pale young woman's own eyes gleaming animatedly in her tired face, and the head nodding as if the knowledge had been there already. It stirred further recollections of her own past.

'You … fancy bein' a cook, do you?' she asked.

Kath nodded hard, then startled Louisa by saying passionately, 'I want to be the best cook in England. I want it more than anything else in the world.'

There followed a long pause, while Louisa collected herself enough from hearing this almost exact echo of her own words to say, 'Well, wanting's half of it.' She roused herself. 'Back to the sink now.'

'Yes'm.'

Kath went, with Louisa's eyes on her. The distant ring of the front doorbell jerked her back into animation again.

'That will be the first of the outside guests,' said Sterling, hurriedly donning his tail coat.

'We're ready when you are,' Louisa replied.

Her confidence underwent a considerable setback some minutes later, though. The order to begin serving up had not yet come. All were poised and ready for it, from Louisa and the major and Mrs Cochrane, to their temporary helpers, Kath and Jennett and Guardsman Wilson. Mr Sterling alone was absent; and now he came hurrying down the stairs to tell Louisa, 'Her ladyship's compliments, Mrs Trotter, but would you put back dinner half an hour, please?'

'It can't be done,' was her emphatic answer. 'Everything's right to the point.'

Unhappily, he explained, 'There's a terrible row going on in the smoking room. It's … Mr Ross, Lady Farjeon's godfather, and Sir John himself and Lord Haslemere. Lady Farjeon has the other guests in the drawing room but they can hear the noise from there. She sounded quite distracted.'

'Right,' Louisa said. 'Mrs Cochrane, you time my soufflé — to the second, mind you. Kath, dish up the consommé. The rest of you, carry on like I told you.' She hitched up her long skirt and ran up the stairs from the kitchen.

'What will she do, Major?' the butler asked Major Smith-Barton.

'Murder, if her dinner's spoiled.'

In the smoking room Charlie was threatening Ross, an aggressive, commanding type of elderly man, 'You repeat that to a living soul and I'll take you through the courts!'

'For God's sake, Charlie!' hissed an almost distraught Major Sir John Farjeon.

'Thank you,' Ross told him smoothly, 'but I'm quite capable of taking care of myself.'

Louisa burst in without knocking, just in time to catch the last words.

'Doesn't sound to me as if any of you's capable of anything,' she snapped, less to the surprise of Haslemere and Farjeon, who knew her of old, than of Ross, who had never set eyes on her. 'Stupid slanging match!' she went on. 'Can't you hear yourselves?'

'May I ask who you are, madam?' Ross demanded.

'This is Mrs Trotter, of the Bentinck Hotel,' Farjeon explained, grim-faced.

Ross smiled and rose to his feet. 'A considerable personality and a distinctive hostelry, or so I'm told. Under other circumstances I'd be pleased to meet you, Mrs Trotter.'

'Yes,' she said, 'and I'm here to do the dinner. Any minute now it's going to spoil. And, having put meself out, I don't intend that it should happen on account of a crowd of men stood there shoutin' the odds. Come on,' she said in a suddenly changed tone, which, again, Haslemere and Farjeon were familiar with, 'you're all grown up. Behave like it. What's it all about?'

Charlie said, as though answering his mother or his nanny, 'Ross accused a friend of mine called Desmond Elleston of cheating.'

'I had it from a racing journalist, who knows,' Ross was stung into defending himself before this female interloper.

'Oh, crikey, newspapers again?' she cried. 'What did he say?'

Charlie answered, 'That Desmond gave orders that his horse shouldn't win the Alexandra Plate this afternoon. The big race.'

'Whyever not? What's he want to chuck that away for?'

'To lengthen the odds for the next race he has the horse entered for — at Goodwood. I say it's unthinkable. Desmond's a gentleman. I've known him all my life.'

But Ross, despite his manner, was arguing from what sounded to Louisa an acceptable standpoint. 'Charles, I'm not complaining because I lost a lot of money I can afford to. We're not talking about someone who's diddled one of his rich friends at cards. If I'm right, Elleston's cheated a lot of poor hopefuls today in order to cheat a lot more at Goodwood. I confess I didn't realise he was such a pal of yours. But if he's done what I say he's done, he doesn't deserve to be.'

'What was this horse called?' asked Louisa, on a sudden instinct.

'Vital Spark,' Farjeon told her. 'What's that to do with it, Louisa?'

She didn't tell him that it had to do with a 'poor hopeful' who dwelt under her own wing, and who was at this moment waiting in the kitchen for the signal to help serve these squabblers from his own class.

'Look,' she told Charlie and Ross. 'You're neither of you goin' to give up till you know the truth, are you?'

'No,' they replied in unison.

'Then find out. Have an unofficial inquiry. Get him here.'

'Desmond would never agree,' Charlie said, aghast at the idea.

'Is he down here?' she persisted.

'Of course. Staying with the Westmacotts.'

'Then invite him over after dinner.'

There was silence for some moments. Then Ross said, 'We'd need an independent arbiter.'

'There's one in this house,' Louisa said. 'Major Smith-Barton, DSO, one-time honorary steward to Calcutta racecourse. Now, what d'you say? Or do I chuck the bleedin' sturgeon in the dustbin and tell the major to drive me 'ome?'

Sir John Farjeon looked at Ross and Charlie. They nodded. He said, 'I'll telephone.'

Lady Farjeon's despairing voice could be heard approaching, pleading for them to come in.

'All right,' he told Louisa. 'I'm sorry. Please start to serve up.'

The dinner went smoothly and all the dishes were well eaten; but those who did the actual serving reported that there was a conspicuous absence of jollity about what had been intended to be a little festivity. At last it was over and word came down that the men, instead of remaining in the dining room alone, had gone into the smoking room, where a caller, Mr Desmond Elleston, had joined them.

To little Kath's surprise, Major Smith-Barton, who, a few minutes before, had been drying dishes as she washed them, was invited to go up and join them. There was report of more raised voices from behind the door.

'Ma'am,' Kath said tentatively to Louisa, who was setting out things for her to heat up for next morning's breakfast, 'what's Mr Elleston doin' here, and all the shoutin'?'

'What do you know about him?' Louisa asked.

'My brother Fred works for him, ma'am. In his stables.'

Louisa was suddenly interested. 'Where Vital Spark's trained?'

'Oh, yes, ma'am. He's goin' to win everythin' sooner or later, Fred says.'

'Well, he doesn't seem to have won today. Between you and me and the gatepost, the row's about someone accusing Mr Elleston of holding the horse back, or whatever they call it, so's he'll get better odds at Goodwood. Daft sport, I reckon.'

But Kath was even more worried now. She was fumbling in her apron pocket for a crumpled letter, which she handed to Louisa.

'Fred sent me this, ma'am. Not that I gamble much … can't afford more than once or twice a year. But he gives me a good tip now and then, and he sent me this letter. Said to save my money on Vital Spark today but have a real go on 'im at Goodwood.'

Louisa read the letter, then turned towards the stairs.

'You're not goin' to take it to 'em?' the maid cried in alarm. 'I don't want to get Fred into trouble.'

'Neither do I, love. I just want to get a pal of mine out of it.'

Her quick ear had detected movement upstairs, and male laughter. There was a convivial note to the men's conversation which reached her as she went up the stairs. The 'inquiry' had just broken up in complete amity. Desmond Elleston had explained what he could only conclude had gone wrong with Vital Spark that day: he blamed himself entirely for instructing his jockey to take up the lead early in the race. Once Vital Spark had done so, and found nothing in front of him to race against, the horse had lost interest and it had been beyond the jockey's capabilities to pull him together again.

'Mr Ross's point,' Major Smith-Barton had put it to him finally, 'is that you now stand to make a fortune if Vital Spark wins at Goodwood.'

'I might just be that far-sighted,' Elleston had agreed. 'Regrettably, though, my creditors aren't, sir. I shall be sold up by then.'

Such candour had proved finally disarming. There had been apologies all round, a final, wholly amicable drink, and now Elleston was leaving, Sir John Farjeon and his guests were about to rejoin the long-suffering ladies, and Major Smith-Barton, DSO, was on his way back to help tidying up the kitchen.

'Thank you, Mrs Trotter,' Ross said, as he encountered her in the hall. 'Your suggestion was an admirable one. Saved us all a scandal. I'm very grateful.'

'That's handsome of you.' She smiled.

Ross added, 'I'm sure Mr Elleston would wish to thank you, too.' He gestured towards that gentleman, who was taking his leave of Charlie Haslemere alone, then bowed and went on his way to the drawing room, where Farjeon had already gone to make their apologies. Louisa went to where the two men were chatting and was introduced by Charlie.

'Liked your tame major immensely,' Desmond Elleston told her. 'Delightful old chap. Tell me, what is he, er, exactly…?'

Her expression surprised him.

'I'll tell you what he is,' she said, in a harsh, low tone. 'He's one of them poor little people you might have took this afternoon, if I hadn't warned him off bettin'. He was one of the lucky ones. I can't make you pay the others back, and if it wouldn't make Charlie here look a proper fool, and upset the Farjeons, then I'd show that Mr Ross this letter here that proves exactly what you meant to do. But you run Vital Spark at Goodwood, and try to take a lot more little people, and I swear I will.'

'You … you're bluffing,' Elleston said. But he had paled, and Charlie was looking at him curiously. 'Let me see that letter.'

'If you see it, the other men do. You know what I'm talkin' about, don't you?'

'You realise I shall go bankrupt,' Elleston said defeatedly.

'That could be the least of your worries. You'll be kicked out of society, the other way, and you'll never get back. And if you want to know, my nice little major *is* bankrupt, or as good as, and could've been worse in it today because of you.'

Without another word Elleston nodded and walked out of the house. Charlie tried to take the crumpled letter from Louisa, but she wouldn't let him have it.

'A bargain's a bargain,' she said.

He replied, stricken, 'I would have gone on oath that that man…'

She smiled. 'You always was a lousy judge of character, love.'

Back in the kitchen she secretly gave the letter back to Kath. 'Burn it,' she said. 'Now. No one's read it, and they'll never know what it was. But it did the trick, thanks.'

The maid hastened to stuff it into the glowing embers of the old range.

'I don't go poachin',' Louisa told her as she did so, 'but if you ever decide to chance your arm up in London, look me up and we'll see what we can do. Eh?'

'Oh, thank you, ma'am!'

'Don't let it go to your head, meantime, though. You make sure they get a nice breakfast. Gawd knows they deserve it.'

She turned to her assistants. Everything was packed up in the 'bus outside.

'Hope we haven't ruined your hands, Miss Jennett,' she told Lady Farjeon's maid. 'And you'd make quite a good footman, if you didn't keep jumpin' to attention,' she chaffed Guardsman Wilson, who grinned back at her and did it again. 'I won't say it's been fun, but we had our moments, didn't we?' Louisa said finally to Mr Sterling, as they shook hands. 'Give my respects to Sir John and Lady Farjeon, will you? I expect he'll be in touch.'

She led her own troops off into the night.

# CHAPTER NINE

'What d'you know about Cowes?' Louisa asked Merriman abruptly in her parlour one morning in the summer of 1909.

Taken somewhat aback, he ventured, 'Cows, ma'am, are large vegetarian mammals. Female — of the bovine species.'

'Oh, blimey! I'm talkin' about rudders, not udders. Tillers and spinnakers and ruddy great yachts. *Cowes* — the sailin' place.'

'I see, ma'am. Well, Lord Haslemere's a member of the Royal Sailing Club there. He's the man to ask about Cowes, I should say.'

'Obviously no use asking you,' Louisa snarled, and turned dismissively back to the page of newspaper on which she had scrawled a circle round an advertisement for a house.

She not only asked Charlie about Cowes; she surprised him by asking him to take her there in his car. He was the newest member of the committee of that august club, and he had to go down for a meeting. She gave no reason for wanting to go, other than a sudden fancy for a day out and a breath of sea air. Charlie, only too pleased to have her company, didn't think to question this uncharacteristic notion.

As they approached the gates of the Royal Yacht Club grounds a certain discomfort which had been growing in him welled up. He swallowed and said nervously, 'I'm awfully sorry, Louisa. I'm not allowed to take you inside.' Louisa, he knew, was not one for being made to seem inferior or obeying anyone's rules but her own. 'Look,' he added hastily, 'I'll see you back here at one o'clock, shall I, and take you for a jolly good luncheon?'

To his surprise and relief, as he stopped the car at the gates bearing the notice STRICTLY PRIVATE. MEMBERS ONLY, Louisa smiled and said, 'That'll be fine. I'll stroll down the prom or something.' She got out and shut the car door. 'Go on. You're late already, aren't you?'

He drove in, saluted by the burly gatekeeper, an ex-Signaller RN named Wilkins. Louisa loitered a moment, surveying the trim premises. Two expensively dressed ladies swept past her without a glance. The gatekeeper saluted again and greeted them deferentially. Wanting to get a better view of the celebrated club, Louisa moved forward to just within the gates. The custodian stepped quickly towards her, frowning aggressively.

'You can't come in here, lady,' he told her, looking her up and down.

'Blimey!' she retorted, her accent confirming his estimate of her class. 'I was only havin' a look.'

'Yeh. Well, do your looking from outside,' he ordered.

Pausing only to regard him in the way she would have looked at a piece of mouldy cheese, Louisa walked away. She did not go far, though. Just next door, in fact, to stand regarding a small house named Rock Cottage. It was the one she had found advertised in the newspaper. After several minutes she smiled and walked briskly away into the town to seek out an address she carried with her.

Charlie Haslemere found that the meeting had started without him. His fellow committee members were Major Gutch, the secretary, a pleasant but anxious man in his late forties; Sir Reginald Blenkiron, a jovial man some years older whose face was not unfamiliar at the Bentinck Hotel; Colonel

Sibley, another Bentinck habitué, who, with Blenkiron, had put up Charlie for the committee; and George Oscroft, a rear admiral in his sixties, of a gruff disposition. The meeting was chaired by the Royal Sailing Club's commodore, Sir Evelyn Grant-Wortley, a crusty old woman-hater. He regarded the latecomer sourly and refused the secretary's suggestion that he read the minutes again for Lord Haslemere's benefit.

'The item under discussion,' the commodore condescended to explain, 'is the desirability or otherwise of purchasing Rock Cottage, the house adjoining these premises — for the benefit of our lady members.' The contempt with which he referred to them left no doubt of his opinion.

Major Gutch told Charlie, 'I put forward an offer agreed at our last meeting, which you couldn't attend. Unfortunately, it was short of the asking price. The question is, do we increase it?'

'Waste of money,' Admiral Oscroft barked.

'But the ladies do have a problem,' Gutch pointed out. 'Nowhere to go if it rains.'

'The marquee,' Oscroft retorted.

'It's only up in regatta week,' Sibley reminded him.

'It's not just the weather,' Blenkiron put in. 'I mean, they're rather stuck on the lawn … for other emergencies.'

Oscroft countered, 'They can use the Strangers' lavatory.'

'Complaints about that. They have to queue up.'

The commodore spoke up. 'We're not having them in the clubhouse, come what may. It's about the last place on earth you can escape from your damn wife — *and* your mistress.'

'Then we've got to get Rock Cottage for them,' Blenkiron said. 'You agree, don't you, Arthur?' he asked Sibley, who nodded vigorously.

'Mutiny otherwise — from my wife, anyway.'

'And we also have to protect ourselves from the possibility of disagreeable neighbours, now old Mrs Crisp's gone.'

This additional argument clinched the matter at last. The commodore commanded the secretary, 'Offer another couple of hundred. They'll accept that. Now, let's get on with the rest.'

While the committee deliberated the problem of a distinguished member and his wife, both in their eighties, who had taken to early-morning bathing from the clubhouse steps, and might thereby set a precedent for others, Rock Cottage was being inspected by Louisa, in the company of the estate agent she had gone into the town to locate. The quite charming little house was unfurnished and rather run down, but it had an irresistible terrace with a superb view out over the water.

'Right on the finishing line of the regatta, Mrs Trotter,' the man told her. 'In Mrs Crisp's day there were the most wonderful parties, I gather. Fairy lights hanging from all the bushes and along here...'

To his astonishment she said simply, 'Right. I'll take it.'

'You mean ... you wish to make an offer, madam?'

'I said I'll take it. Something wrong?'

'No, no. Only ... we have had another enquiry. I ought not to divulge ... well, it's from the Royal Sailing Club next door. We're just waiting for them to come back with a better figure.'

Still smarting at her exclusion from that establishment, and the gatekeeper's manner towards her, Louisa said firmly, 'Look, I'm offerin' you the full price. Cash.'

She opened the large handbag she was carrying and held it towards him. The estate agent's eyes widened at the sight of tied-up bundles of banknotes.

Charlie was horrified when she met him and told him casually what she'd done.

'You can't!' he protested. 'We've just decided to buy it.'

'Should've been quicker off the mark, then, shouldn't you?'

'You mean you just walked in and…'

'No. Saw it advertised in the paper. That's why I asked for a lift down.'

'You mean you took advantage of me, and now…! Oh, Lord, when the committee hear about our … connection they'll think I put you up to it.'

'So what? Some of my best clients are members of your snobby old club. Reggie Blenkiron, old Saffron Walden … they'll be happy to have me near.'

'They might, but their wives won't. The ladies of the club have set their hearts on the cottage.'

'Too bad for 'em. Look, Charlie, whose side are you on? You should be pleased as Punch. Nice little place to come and stay. We'll liven the place up a bit, too. I reckon we'll have a real housewarming, soon as I've got some furniture in.'

The furnishing process did not take long. Meanwhile, Louisa gave all the Bentinck's residents and guests notice that she would be taking two months' holiday and that most of her staff would be accompanying her, including Mrs Cochrane, the cook, Merriman, Starr, and the maid, Ethel. Mary Philips and Major Smith-Barton would supervise the hotel and meals would continue to be provided by the kitchen assistants, though not on any elaborate scale.

Then the day came when she and her retainers, together with an amiable but impoverished marquis, Tommy Shepherd, and his red-haired widow friend, Mrs Delaney, piled into the hotel 'bus and were driven off by Starr, with Fred sitting up beside him. Champagne was, of course, drunk throughout the journey, and when the party eventually debussed at Cowes their steps were unsteady and their voices loud.

A band on the Sailing Club lawn was playing Gilbert and Sullivan. Teaspoons were tinkling in saucers like extra instruments. The arrival of some noisy persons at Rock Cottage did not go unremarked, and there were exchanges of outraged looks between the members' ladies when some raucous singing was heard. Lady Blenkiron, Mrs Sibley and one or two others so far departed from decorum as to stand on their wicker chairs and look over the hedge. Louisa saw them and grinned. 'Wotcher, ladies!' she greeted them.

At that moment Tommy Shepherd dashed into view, whooping with mock fear as Mrs Delaney pursued him with a croquet mallet. The watchers' heads disappeared like a row of knocked-down coconuts.

'Who are those dreadful people?' Lady Blenkiron demanded.

Hugo 'Saffron' Walden, who was smiling, answered with what sounded like glee, 'Louisa Trotter and guests, dear lady. She's taken the cottage.'

Lady Blenkiron glared at her husband, who was not openly sharing his bachelor friend's enjoyment of the prospect. She said accusingly, 'You informed me categorically that the house would be *ours*.'

'My dear, I told you we were outbid. The club funds couldn't enable us to go over the full price.'

'I've heard the woman runs a brothel,' Mrs Sibley said shockingly.

'Oh, no,' her own husband answered. 'It's a jolly nice place.'

'You mean to say you've been there?'

'I, er … well, everyone stays there at some time or another. I mean, members of parliament … the king, in his time…'

'Hm!' Mrs Sibley's suspicions were even deeper now.

'Clergy, too,' Blenkiron hastened to say. 'Lots of 'em.'

Major Gutch, who had been keeping out of it, felt he should make some official utterance. 'I assure you, ladies,' he said, 'we shall be keeping a careful eye on the situation. If we feel a complaint is justified, we shall not hesitate to make one.'

'I think there is little doubt that you will be doing,' Lady Blenkiron said. 'Great heavens, what next? A dog loose on our lawn!'

Fred, impelled by curiosity, had entered the grounds at a moment when Wilkins, the gatekeeper, had not been looking. Wilkins had seen him now and was advancing fast. Fred looked all round, his features bearing no sign that he was impressed. He wandered over to a basket chair, cocked a leg up to it, then nonchalantly trotted away back to friendlier territory, calmly eluding Wilkins as he went.

The housewarming party took place two nights later. Coloured fairy lights were once more in profusion in the small garden of Rock Cottage and along the terrace, adding to the romantic effect of the riding-lights of the moored yachts. Several of Louisa's friends had travelled specially down from London, and there was no let-up for Merriman in his rounds with the champagne bottles.

Charlie Haslemere was there. So, also, was a very special catch of Louisa's: Irene Baker, the current toast of the West End musical stage.

'How on earth did you get her?' Charlie had asked, when Louisa had told him Irene would be coming to stay with her. 'Half of London must be offering her yachts and villas, now that her show's just closed.'

'I just asked her,' Louisa said casually. 'She was in the hotel with someone before we left, and I asked her. Mentioned you might be here, and she seemed to jump at it.'

He looked at her suspiciously, but her face gave nothing away.

Now, arriving late at the party after dining on someone's yacht, Charlie found Irene on a sofa, appearing, to judge from their positions, to have been edging unsuccessfully away from 'Saffron' Walden.

'Charles, dear boy,' Walden greeted him, 'I was just saying to Miss Baker that her dance in the second act was like a bright star in a horribly dull season. Wouldn't you agree?'

Charlie took Irene's hand. 'I can't remember a more intensely enjoyable evening in the theatre,' he said sincerely.

'Thank you,' she said, 'I can't remember a nicer compliment.'

Their hands stayed in one another's. Walden sighed and got up. 'See I'm superfluous,' he said, and wandered off with his empty glass in pursuit of Merriman.

Charlie sat down next to Irene. She didn't edge away from him. Their thighs touched and stayed. She was very beautiful: beautifully dressed, beautifully perfumed...

'I was hoping I might have seen you again ... after that party at Romano's,' she told him candidly.

'You were surrounded by admirers. I felt my chances were slim, to say the least.'

'You should have had more faith.'

Charlie felt his heart leap. 'How ... how long are you staying?' he almost blurted out.

'I've three weeks before my next rehearsals start.'

'But that's marvellous! *Will* you stay? Have you ever been sailing?'

She shook her head. 'I used to stand on the beach, as a child, and watch the yachts go by, and dream that someday... Of course, I've got a lot of offers now, though.'

Charlie told her delightedly, 'Then I claim the privilege of being the one who fulfils your dream for you. If you'll allow me, that is?'

She gazed into his eyes and nodded slowly.

In the kitchen Merriman told Starr and Mrs Cochrane, 'She's set her compass at his lordship, and no mistake.'

'What does Mrs Trotter seem to think about it?' the cook asked.

'Seems to be encouraging them.'

'Waste of time.' Starr said. 'She'd never make a lady in a hundred years. Her father's a jobbing builder at Bognor.'

'Lady or not,' Ethel said, coming in and hearing this, 'I wish I had a body like hers.'

When Merriman got back to the terrace with yet another bottle of champagne he found Lord Haslemere and Irene Baker with their backs to him, taking it in turns to peer through a long brass telescope on a mounting. It was tilted skywards. There was silence in the house now. All the other guests had gone and Mrs Trotter had disappeared.

'Uranus, I think,' his lordship was saying. 'Or is it the Pole Star?'

'I don't believe you know one from another,' the beautiful actress giggled. They were shoulder to shoulder and his arm was about her slender waist. Merriman retreated silently behind the curtains and uncorked the bottle there with an unnecessary pop. They had stood apart by the time he went out to them.

'Thank you, Merriman,' Lord Haslemere said. 'Don't wait up for me. I'll turn out the lights.'

Merriman took polite leave of them. When he had gone, Irene was about to move to Charlie again. He stopped her with a gesture.

'Don't move. The moon had caught you perfectly. On stage, I thought you were the most divine apparition I'd ever seen. Off stage, I find you … even more divine. Irene…!'

He didn't restrain her this time as she came forward into his arms and to a long, passionate kiss, after which she murmured into his shoulder, 'And I've imagined somebody like you all my life.'

The next morning, Louisa did a rare thing for her: she went for a walk with no more purpose than to enjoy the air. Preferring to chat rather than to keep silent, she looked for Charlie to accompany her, but was told he was still asleep. So she commanded Starr to go with her; and, of course, Fred went too, trotting happily a few paces ahead, weaving from side to side and enjoying a whole new range of smells.

'Not so bad, this fresh air lark,' Louisa remarked contentedly.

'The air is surprisingly bracing, madam,' Starr answered.

A middle-aged couple approaching them smiled and nodded to Louisa and went on.

'That's Lord Pembury,' she told Starr. 'Bit before your time. If his wife knew what I know about him she wouldn't be lookin' so pleased with herself.'

Another couple were approaching now. Both were ladies, and Louisa recognised them as the pair who had passed her at the Sailing Club gates, and whose faces had been amongst those peering outraged over the hedge into her garden.

'Momin', ladies!' she greeted them cheerfully.

They stuck their noses into the air. 'Don't answer,' the beefier of them said to the other, deliberately loudly.

'I wouldn't presume to,' replied the companion.

'Every bit as common as she looks,' came floating back to Louisa when the women had gone by. 'I can't think what Cowes is coming to. Brothel-keepers now.'

Starr, who had also heard, took the liberty of clutching at his employer's arm just in time to prevent her turning and running after the women to give them an extended sample of Covent Garden argot.

'No, no, ma'am,' he pleaded. 'I beg you, don't rise to it!'

His persuasion worked, but Louisa's taste for strolling was gone. She stormed back to Rock Cottage with Starr hurrying beside her and Fred no longer allowed to keep pausing on the way. She found Charlie and Irene in the garden.

'What's happened?' Charlie asked, recognising one of Louisa's furies from well-known signs.

'I've been insulted, that's what's happened. By so-called ladies from your club. Called me a brothel-keeper. Well, I want their names. One's built like a 'bus — wears a wig and a hat with tomatoes on it…'

Charlie took care not to smile. 'That sounds like Rose Blenkiron,' he said. 'She generally goes about with Mrs Sibley. But I'd ignore them, Louisa.'

'No bloody fear! I don't ignore personal injuries — you should know that. It's war!'

The roulette party Louisa proceeded to throw that evening was surpassingly noisy. She encouraged those guests who were not preoccupied with the wheel and the counters to join her in singing lusty choruses of music-hall ditties of the broadest nature. Fuelled by her champagne, they complied willingly, including those of them who were respected members of the club next door, where their wives believed they were playing a quiet game of bridge.

The following day the Commodore of the Royal Sailing Club summoned Charlie to his presence in the library. The band was playing something vaguely pastoral on the lawn, where the ladies were mustered as usual.

'This woman friend of yours next door, Haslemere,' Sir Evelyn Grant-Wortley began without preamble. 'You know her pretty well, they tell me.'

'Mrs Trotter?' Charlie answered coolly. 'Yes, I do.'

'And you told her to buy that cottage?'

'Certainly not. I'd no idea…'

'Well, that's not what I've heard. Anyway, she's causing trouble. Complaints from members. Noise.'

'Really?' Charlie replied innocently. He had been present the previous evening, though he had spent most of it exclusively in the company of Irene Baker.

'Tell her to pipe down or get out,' the commodore ordered.

Imagining the outcome of his undertaking any such hazard, Charlie said, 'Sir Evelyn, I really don't think it's my business personally.'

'What? Dammit, you can hear her now.'

They could indeed. Shrieks and bellows of laughter were coming from across the hedge. Charlie could just imagine what was going on — an un-serious croquet game between Tommy Shepherd and Mrs Delaney, with suggestive prompts from the champagne-bibbers.

As he and the commodore went to the window to see for themselves, Lady Blenkiron, losing all restraint, got up on to her chair on the lawn again and roared at the Rock Cottage people, 'Will you keep quiet over there!'

'You keep yer band quiet!' Louisa's voice was heard to yell back.

'Oh, lor'!' the commodore moaned at Charlie's side. 'More trouble coming from the blasted women. Had enough already.'

He and Charlie watched Lady Blenkiron clamber down and march over to the bandmaster. She shouted something forceful up at him. He gave a little bow of acknowledgment, rounded off the number they were playing, gave some instructions to the players, then, raising his baton high, crashed them into a march tune.

Retaliation was not long forthcoming. To Charlie's horrified disbelief an upper window of Rock Cottage was pushed open a few minutes later and there hurtled out of it a missile which crashed on to the Sailing Club lawn, near to Lady Blenkiron's table. It was white in colour and fragile in texture, for it smashed into several pieces, which flew about dangerously. It was followed by another and another. Though all shattered where they fell amongst the cowering ladies there was no difficulty for the men at the library window in identifying them as chamber pots.

Cries of 'Outrage!', 'Scandalous!' and even 'Police!' arose from the ladies as they scattered.

'My God!' the commodore groaned, and hurried away to hide.


'It was unforgivable!' Charlie scolded Louisa later. He was really annoyed with her. 'What on earth possessed you?'

'They asked for it.'

'No, they didn't. Don't you realise you could have injured someone seriously? Some of those old ladies have matchstick bones.'

Louisa was unrepentant. 'They're askin' for conveniences, aren't they? Well, I gave 'em some chamber pots.'

'It isn't a joke, Louisa. The commodore's furious now, and with good reason. He wants an immediate apology.'

'I'm not apologisin' —'

'You *are* apologising. Your behaviour was stupid, dangerous and damned irresponsible.'

He had never spoken to her like this before. The fact registered, despite her own anger. She countered resentfully, 'Well, your behaviour hasn't been much to write home about, these past few days.'

'What's that supposed to mean?'

'Don't look so innocent. You and Miss bloody Baker.'

'Louisa, that's extremely unfair. You practically threw us together — in fact, I think you did it deliberately.'

'Well, you don't have to make such a meal out of it.'

'Oh, for God's sake…! Irene and I are just having fun together. I mean, she's awfully sweet, and…'

'You goin' to marry her?' Louisa asked with a directness which startled him into pausing before answering.

'Of … course I'm not,' he said at first; then amended it to, 'At least, I don't think so.' After a further pause he asked in his more familiar schoolboy manner, 'Would you mind if I did?'

Louisa shrugged. 'It's your life. Do what you like.'

He surprised her by saying, 'I could never do that … never marry anyone … without your approval, Louisa. To be quite honest, I was looking on Irene as a sort of blow for freedom.'

'What's that supposed to mean?'

'Well, to help separate *us*. It must happen one day — mustn't it? I thought she was a sort of present from you, for that purpose. I was rather touched.'

Irene appeared in the doorway at that moment. 'Are you coming now?' she asked Charlie. 'I'm ready for town.'

He looked at Louisa, who hadn't moved. 'Just a moment, my angel,' he told Irene. 'See you in a moment.'

Irene hesitated, then went. Charlie told Louisa quietly, 'Look, all in all, perhaps it's best if I leave here.'

'Why?'

'I just do.'

She roused herself. 'You can't. You can't leave me to the mercy of your old Wort-Grantly, or whatever he calls himself.'

'Oh, yes. I'd forgotten that. He wants to see you, and I'm expected to arrange it.'

'He can always pop round here, or ask me to his place.'

'He's hardly likely to do either of those. We'll have to find some common ground. I know — Blenkiron's yacht. I'll fix it for tomorrow.'

Louisa shook her head. 'I'm not going there, Charlie. Not with that wife of his within spittin' distance. I wouldn't trust myself.'

He spoke firmly again, but smiled this time and laid his hand on her arm: 'You'll do as you're told.'

And so the next afternoon found Louisa, escorted by Sir Reginald Blenkiron and Charlie, descending the steps into the luxurious saloon of the Blenkiron yacht, advancing towards the frosty stares of Sir Evelyn Grant-Wortley, Admiral Oscroft and Lady Blenkiron, and the apologetic little welcoming smile of Major Gutch. The men all rose. Lady Blenkiron remained seated, rock-like.

Cold introductions were made. Major Gutch suggested, 'Won't you sit down, Mrs Trotter?' and gave her a chair. She favoured him alone with a smile.

The commodore cleared his throat. 'Mrs Trotter —' he began his prepared address, but she interrupted him with a rush.

'I will apologise. But only if she does first.' She jerked her head towards Lady Blenkiron, without looking at her. That lady bridled.

'Apologise? For what?'

'She knows,' Louisa told the commodore, still without looking at her.

Charlie stepped in. 'Perhaps I can explain? Mrs Trotter believes that she heard Lady Blenkiron utter a rather damaging remark about her in public, while she was walking on the promenade.'

'I heard it, all right,' Louisa affirmed. 'And I've a witness.'

'What rubbish!' Lady Blenkiron retorted.

Louisa addressed her directly for the first time. 'Care to deny it in a court of law?'

Admiral Oscroft intervened, 'What's all this to do with throwing chamber pots?

Major Gutch said, 'I think what Lord Haslemere is intimating is that the remark might perhaps have precipitated the, er, pot incident.'

'Now there's a clever feller,' Louisa said, smiling at the club secretary again. He smiled nervously back and glanced furtively at the others, most of whom shot him looks of disfavour.

'Mrs Trotter,' Lady Blenkiron said, 'I must ask you to remember that you are a guest aboard my yacht.'

'Look,' Louisa proceeded to lecture her in turn, 'I didn't ask to come here, and I didn't expect any inquisition, neither. I'd have been happy to talk this whole thing out at my cottage over a glass of wine. But since we are met here, let's get a few things straight. I buy a house in what's supposed to be a free country, mind me own business, and find myself bloomin' insulted left, right and centre, just because I have a few friends — half of 'em your members, by the way — who like their bit of fun. There's always been parties there in the past, I've been told. Now, if it's all a campaign to get me out, just so's your ladies can have somewhere to have a … to relieve themselves, that's another matter.'

She returned her look towards the commodore and addressed him. 'Personally, I feel sorry for 'em, poor creatures, the way you lot treat 'em. I wouldn't stand for it if I belonged to your bloomin' club. But the fact is, I'm not budgin', so there's got to be give and take on both sides.'

'If I might put in a word…' the commodore began again, but he and the other men were astonished by the nature of Lady Blenkiron's interruption.

'She's right.'

'I … I beg your pardon?'

'I said, Mrs Trotter's right. The club wives *are* treated abominably. It's quite like the Middle Ages. What do you propose to do about it, Commodore?'

'My dear Lady Blenkiron…'

'No. Sweet words are not going to be enough. Action is what is needed. Mrs Trotter mentioned give and take on both sides. I for one should be most interested to hear what she has in mind.'

'I'll tell you,' Louisa answered. 'I'm prepared to sell your club the annexe to my house — for the ladies only.'

'Waste of money,' Admiral Oscroft grunted. 'Managed for fifty years without.'

'"Managed" is hardly the word, George,' Lady Blenkiron rebuked him. 'Have you ever been in the Strangers' lavatory?'

'Mrs Trotter,' the commodore intervened, clutching at the straw of hope, 'may we take it, then, that you will sell us your annexe?'

'Yes,' Louisa said. 'But only on condition that…'

The following afternoon Charlie and Irene stood facing one another in the cottage sitting room.

'Must you really go?' she pouted.

'Yes, really. Estate business to attend to, and so forth.'

'But you haven't taken me sailing yet.'

'I'll arrange for someone to take you out. There'll be no shortage of volunteers. In any case, I'll try to come back … next weekend. And I'll write every day.'

His instincts were genuinely pulling him in opposite directions. She sensed that he was experiencing some difficulties.

'You haven't got tired of me?' she asked, watching his eyes closely. He managed not to let his gaze falter.

'No. Oh, no. I adore you.'

She pushed herself into his arms and they kissed passionately again, he just as eagerly as she. They were interrupted by a commotion of voices from outside the house and then the hurried entry of Tommy Shepherd.

'Oh, awfully sorry,' he exclaimed. 'Only … there's a most amazing thing happening out there. Do come and look.'

Hand in hand, Charlie and Irene followed him on to the lawn. Mrs Delaney was pointing excitedly out over the water. They shaded their eyes and looked.

The pinnace of the Commodore of the Royal Sailing Club was nearing shore. In its bows stood the commodore. But he occupied a position of deference, a pace behind another figure — Louisa.

Leaving his friends, Charlie dashed from the cottage to the club gates, where to his astonishment he found a strip of red carpet, reserved for royal visits, laid. Several of his fellow members, including Sir Reginald Blenkiron, Colonel Sibley, Admiral Oscroft and 'Saffron' Walden were lined up, together with their club secretary, Major Gutch, to form a reception committee. Wilkins, the gatekeeper, came stiffly to attention as the pinnace touched the steps and the commodore personally handed Louisa ashore.

Charlie, who had, of course, heard the conditions of sale she had laid down, but hadn't expected them to be taken seriously, stepped hastily into line with the rest. From the corner of his eye he saw the ladies rising in amazement from their chairs to get a better view of the incredible proceedings. The band, which had been playing something insipid, struck up 'Rule Britannia'.

Like a queen, the duchess of Duke Street proceeded along the red carpet, accepting Wilkins's salute with a gracious inclination of her head and bestowing a nod and a smile of greeting to each member in turn. When she found Charlie at the end of the line she paused, just momentarily, to say, 'Blow for freedom, eh, Charlie?'

Then she went on, straight into the clubhouse, to become the first woman ever to be entertained there to tea. The first had been Queen Victoria. Louisa Trotter had won yet another of life's battles.

# CHAPTER TEN

Having waited so long for the throne, and for the authority to be seen to be ruling his people so far as any modern constitutional monarch could do so, Edward VII worked tirelessly to make up for the frustrating inactivity of his first sixty years. But although he achieved much, the chance had come too late. Enforced idleness and luxurious living had undermined his health permanently. For years he had carried a great excess of weight, eating, drinking and smoking far too much than was good for him. These abuses had inevitably affected his heart and lungs.

The year 1909 — his sixty-eighth — proved to be the most stressful of his reign. The triumph of the visit to Germany and the elation at winning the Derby were soon eclipsed by the political crisis engendered by the high-handed new Chancellor of the Exchequer, Lloyd George. His budget was almost calculated to incur the veto of the House of Lords, thus providing the excuse to abolish that House altogether or at least so to pack it with newly created Liberal peers that it would be powerless to oppose the government's measures. In his speech at the opening of Parliament, in which he could only pass on his government's proposals, whatever he felt about them, Edward was careful to say that he was merely expressing the opinion of his advisers. Had he heeded the opinion of those other advisers responsible for his health, the following year, 1910, might have turned out rather differently for him.

In the event, though, he had a further severe attack of bronchitis, followed by a series of heart attacks. On top of the work, the worry, and the overweight, they were enough to kill him. They did, on May 6th.

'That Asquith killed him,' declared Louisa of the Prime Minister, who had been booed to that effect in the streets by crowds shattered at the loss of their popular monarch.

Louisa was addressing Starr in the Bentinck's hall. She was dressed all in black. The news of the death had staggered her as much as it had anyone, and more than most. Memories, surprisingly tender memories, had swept over her like a flood tide when she had been told. She had not seen him for the past few years, and their intimate relationship had been brief and long ago. She was not an emotional woman, but time had deepened her affection for him and she had followed his triumphant career with personal pride. The fact that he had been so gravely ill had not been made public, so that his death had had all the more impact. It was as if he had been snuffed out like a candle still only half burnt.

Starr wore a black crepe armband. Even his dog had his crepe mourning collar.

'Lord Henry Norton's come to see you, ma'am,' Starr told Louisa, who had just come in. 'I took the liberty of putting him in your room.'

Louisa was surprised. It was some years, too, since Lord Henry, in whose service she had first met the late king, had been in touch with her, although Charlie Haslemere, his nephew, referred to him from time to time. Merriman was crossing the hall. She ordered him, 'Bottle of wine in my room, if you please. And four glasses.'

'Yes, madam.' He had long known better than to ask what sort of wine she desired. It was invariably champagne — the best.

She found Lord Henry examining the many photographs of favourite hotel guests, mostly male, which almost papered the walls of her littered parlour-cum-office: men in uniform of all kinds, in hunting clothes, polo outfits, yachting blazers and caps and other sporting rig. He, too, wore mourning clothes.

He smiled and shook hands with her. 'How are you, Louisa?' She was surprised to hear him use her Christian name. 'Sad news, eh? One less for your gallery, I'm afraid.' He gestured to the framed photograph of Edward.

She nodded wistfully. 'And the most important one. If it hadn't been for him I mightn't be here now. Still your assistant cook, eh, Lord Henry?'

'I often wish you were. But we were both lucky. The king honoured us with his friendship. But it's quite extraordinary how all the people one sees in the street look so sad.'

'He was their friend, too,' Louisa said. 'The finest gentleman I ever ran up against — present company excepted, of course.' She sat down, and rubbed her thighs. 'I'm creaking. Been on me knees across at the church in Piccadilly. Bought a black dress, too. I wouldn't have done either for anyone else.'

Merriman knocked and entered with the champagne. When he had opened it she ordered him to call Starr in and come back himself. He did, and poured two glasses, then hesitated.

'Go on,' Louisa commanded. 'You two take a glass as well.'

Merriman poured again. Then Louisa proposed a toast. Her voice quavered slightly. 'Here's to the memory of King Edward the Seventh. May God bless him where 'e's gone.'

The strangely assorted quartet — peer of the realm, hotel proprietress, hall porter and ancient waiter — drank together gravely. Then Louisa jerked her head and Starr and Merriman retired. 'What's the new bloke like?' she asked Lord Henry, referring, of course, to His Majesty King George the Fifth.

'I hardly know him,' he answered. 'Nice, quiet respectable married man. Very naval, I gather.'

'Not particularly likely to patronise this place, then,' she laughed. 'Charlie Haslemere wired. He's coming up today.'

'Yes, I know.'

'I haven't seen him for months … what with his huntin' and fishin'.'

'Yes,' Lord Henry said, seeming to accept this as an opportunity to say what he had come to say. 'That, er, is what I wanted to talk to you about really, Louisa. You see, I'm now his only surviving relative. Near relative, that is. *In loco parentis* sort of thing, don't you know? It's a bit of a responsibility — the estate and, ah, so forth…'

Louisa smiled again. 'So you think he oughter stop sowing all them wild oats and start doing a bit of harvesting? Settle down?'

'Exactly,' Lord Henry replied, relieved.

'Well, I can do a lot of things for him, but I don't think I can find him a wife.'

'Oh, no, no. But I think … I, ah, hope *I* have.'

This jolted Louisa somewhat. Charlie might be no more to her emotionally nowadays than the late king had been, and she had long since grown accustomed to cooking for him and his married lady friends, knowing full well what they would be up to when the dinner things had been removed. But the thought of his marrying had been so remote from her mind that it came as a little shock. 'Oh … good,' was all she could say.

'Very nice girl,' Lord Henry went on. 'Parents both dead, sadly. Nice family, though.'

'That's good, then. I hope he'll be happy. But it's not my concern, is it?'

'Oh yes, it is, Louisa. I'm very fond of Charles, as you know, and I know him pretty well. I also know that there's no one in the world he admires and respects as much as you. You, ah, know what I'm talking about?'

'Yeh, I know,' Louisa said, twigging that he was referring to her and Charlie's baby. 'Well, I won't do anything to muck it up, don't worry. That is, if I think they're suited.'

Lord Henry looked at her with sharp suspicion.

'Is he very bitten with her?' she asked.

'Well … it's not quite the same as…'

He was interrupted before he could make any further allusion, however oblique, to the short-lived relationship between her and his nephew by the entry of the latter himself.

'Caught you at it, by George!' Charlie said accusingly to his uncle, who looked startled. 'Drinking at this hour,' he added with a grin.

Lord Henry relaxed again, getting up from the chair on which he had been seated. 'Bad luck for you, we've finished the bottle,' he said. 'I must be off. You're dining with me tonight, Charles, and don't you forget. The Keppels and the Farjeons are coming, so it'll be rather gloomy, I'm afraid. All down in the dumps just now. Wish you were doing the dinner, Louisa. Got a temperamental Italian feller as chef nowadays. Can hear him screaming his head off in the library. Poor old Mrs Catchpole's going into a decline, too.'

He shook hands with Louisa and went. She turned to Lord Haslemere and regarded him. He came forward, smiling, and gave her the usual chaste but fond kiss.

'Haven't seen you for a bit,' she said, feeling awkward. 'Been behavin' yourself, like a good boy?'

'You know me,' he said lightly, but she could sense his unease. 'Louisa, I've … got someone coming to tea.'

'That's all right. You just have to ring the bell in your room, same as usual.'

'I think it would be better if we had it in the hall.'

'Please yourself.'

'You see, it's a girl.'

'Oooh! Now you do shock me, you really do, Lord Haslemere.'

'Louisa, be serious, please. You see, she's a rather quietly brought up sort of girl. She wouldn't understand it if we had tea in my rooms. I mean, without a chaperone.'

'Knowing you, she might learn a thing or two,' Louisa persisted with the banter. But he went on seriously, embarrassed.

'Will you be … I mean, will you be very careful? Er, watch what you say — your language?'

She would have taken instant offence at this, coming from anyone else, and it did sting her, even from him. 'Crikey!' she exclaimed. 'If her ears are that delicate, why don't you take her to Gunter's, where she won't be corrupted?'

'Louisa, I particularly want you to meet Mar — Miss Wormald. She's … a girl I met up in Scotland. She's awfully good at fishing. Likes walking… She's an orphan. Actually, Sir James Rosslyn's her guardian.'

'Oh, old Rosy!' she exclaimed, recalling the senior Liberal politician, another person she had not encountered for quite some time.

'Living down in Dorset most of the year, she's had, well, rather a dull sort of life,' Charlie concluded his pathetic attempt to prepare the ground. Louisa knew perfectly well what he was doing, but spared him any blunt questioning in the light of what Lord Henry had told her. The woman sounded to her hearty and heavily county, hardly Charlie's usual type at all. 'I do hope you'll like her,' he ended.

'All right. I'll put on me best bib and tucker and mind me ps and qs — and a few other letters.'

'Thanks. Oh, by the way, she particularly likes chocolate éclairs.'

'There's none made.'

'Please — Louisa.'

'Oh, bleedin' hell. I wish you'd stayed put where you was.'

There was more unconscious meaning in that than either of them recognised. He merely thanked her and went away.

That afternoon Louisa looked on as Margaret Wormald tasted her first mouthful of éclair at the table beside the hall fireplace. She was a pretty enough young woman, in her early twenties: demure, in an old-fashioned way, which her rather dull clothes complemented exactly.

'I think that's just the best éclair I've ever tasted!' she exclaimed, as soon as her mouth was empty.

'Louisa — Mrs Trotter — made them herself,' Charles Haslemere told her.

She looked up at the impassive Louisa with awe. 'You mean … *you* cooked them, Mrs Trotter?'

'With me own fair hands.'

'I … I didn't know you cooked as well.'

'I don't, as much as I used to. Only when it's something special.'

The young woman seemed surprised to be regarded as 'something special'. Louisa nodded, by way of confirmation, and said, 'Well, if you'll excuse me, I've got the menus to see to.' She went off to her room.

'What a funny woman!' Margaret Wormald said to Charlie, pouring him more tea. 'Such a common voice.'

'Yes,' he had to agree. 'But a very good cook. A great one.'

'And you always stay here when you're in town?'

'That's right. I've got permanent rooms. You must come up and see them sometime.'

'Uncle James stayed here once. I think he found it rather … noisy.'

'Oh? Really?'

At that moment Sir James Rosslyn himself came through the front door. He, too, wore mourning. He glanced round and espied the couple at their table.

'Hullo, Haslemere,' he greeted Charlie, who rose and shook hands. 'Come to take this young lady away from you. Going to a lecture at the Royal Society — on volcanoes.'

'Hello, Sir Rosy!' they heard Louisa's approaching voice. 'You Liberals not so cocky now, eh? Majority of only two, wasn't it?'

'Not good,' he agreed, shaking hands.

'Nobody's fault but your own,' she told him bluntly. 'That Winston Churchill's a nice boy and appreciates my cooking, but he thinks with his mouth. And as for Lloyd George and this People's Budget of his — you'll ruin us all.'

'Perfectly sound fiscal measure,' he disagreed. 'We'll get it through once we've scotched those half-baked Conservative peers. Oh, beg pardon, Haslemere.'

'Don't mind me,' Charlie laughed. 'Here you see the most unpolitical Conservative peer in captivity.'

'That's where most of 'em should be,' Louisa said. 'Behind bars at the zoo.'

Her opinion of Margaret Wormald rose a little when that young lady said, with sudden spirit, 'We could go and feed them all with buns.'

'Louisa's éclairs, please,' Charlie said.

They all laughed, then Sir James, who had a taxi waiting, took Margaret away, promising to return her safely.

'He don't change much — dry old stick,' Louisa said to Charlie.

'He treats her as if she were still about fourteen,' he replied. He glanced round the hall, then said, 'I say, Louisa, could you spare a minute? In your room?'

'Of course, love,' she consented. As they passed the desk she ordered Starr, 'Tell old Dundrearyman to fetch a bottle to my room.'

'Yes, ma'am,' he answered. '"Old Dundrearyman",' he repeated to Fred, who trotted after him towards the dispense in search of Merriman. 'Shall we tell him she called him that, eh?'

In Louisa's parlour Charlie stammered, uncertain how to say what he wanted to say, so Louisa said it for him.

'You want to know if you should pop the question to your little Miss Wormygold, is that it? Wondering whether she's the right one for you at last.'

'How the devil...?' he gaped.

'Oh, Charlie, love, I can read you like an open book. Always could. But why ask me this one?'

'Well, you're the only person I've ever asked to marry me so far. Isn't that a good enough recommendation?'

'I dunno,' she sighed. 'I mean, how well d'you know her?'

'Well, we met quite often in Scotland.'

'All by yourselves, was you?'

'No. Never.' After a pause he added, 'She's quite jolly, really. Not half such a mouse as…'

'You don't have to apologise for her.'

'No. The trouble is — it's damn difficult to get to know someone like Margaret. Properly, I mean.'

'*We* managed to get to know each other, all right.'

'Oh, but that's not possible. I mean, I couldn't…'

'She bein' a lady,' Louisa couldn't help retorting cattily.

'That's unfair!' he protested.

'Yes, it was,' Louisa had to agree.'You always treated me like a lady, though I wasn't one, I'll give you that.'

Merriman came in with the champagne. She was able to take her discomfiture out on him.

'Been over to France to get it, have you? Just leave it for 'is lordship to open. You hop off and die somewhere.'

Accustomed and impervious to her insults, the old man put down the tray and tottered out. Charlie opened the bottle and poured for them both. They drank a little private toast, each remembering old times. He gave her one of his light kisses.

'Can't see no stars in your eyes, Charlie,' she sighed. 'You're not head over heels, that's for sure.'

'No, I'm not. But don't you think it better … or might be better … just to start off liking each other?'

'And then, as time goes by, getting fonder and fonder? Like it was a piece of furniture, or a dog, or something?' He shrugged uncertainly. She had to help him as best she could. 'She looks healthy enough, and the big idea's to produce a future little Lord Haslemere, I suppose?'

'Frankly, yes.'

'Then she's a lucky girl, Charlie.'

'You think I should, then?'

'Why not? You pays yer money…'

'That is, if she'll have me.'

'Or if Sir Rosy will have you.'

He stared at her. This hadn't entered his mind. But when he went to call on Sir James Rosslyn at the first opportunity for a formal talk, next day, he soon found that Louisa's point had been a cogent one.

'I do want you to see it from my point of view, Haslemere,' the fastidious older man said, when the preliminaries were over and Charlie had made his request without receiving a direct answer. 'Margaret's parents were my very, very dear friends. She was their only child. I'm not only her guardian, but her trustee. She is my greatest responsibility in the world. I think I feel more responsible for her than her actual parents would — that is to say, if they were still alive.'

Charlie noted to himself that the man's pomposity certainly hadn't decreased with the years. He decided to cut short the homily.

'And I clearly don't meet with your approval,' he said.

'I didn't say that. I didn't say that at all. But we can be frank with each other. In fact, we *must* be frank. You have, er, ah, a reputation. A certain reputation for … how shall I put it…?'

'Being a flibbertigibbet.'

'A what?'

'No matter.'

'Hm. You see, Haslemere, I don't like rumours. But there was at one time something of a rumour that you and … and Louisa Trotter…'

'Sir James,' Charlie interrupted quickly, 'I like women and women seem to like me. I'm lucky to have lots of friends and plenty of money. So I've had a very jolly ten or so enjoying myself.'

'That's exactly what I mean. Your character is rather … light, if I may say so. You haven't cared to take on any responsibility. Politics. Justice of the Peace…' He sighed. 'However, I must admit that Margaret seems very fond of you. Only, she's seen very little of life.'

'Whose fault is that?' Charlie couldn't help riposting, but Sir James Rosslyn was not one for self-criticism.

'I've done my duty as I've seen fit,' he said stiffly. 'And, having said my piece, I must tell you that if the marriage settlement arrangements are suitable, as I am sure they will be, I do not feel I should stand in your way. So you have my blessing.'

He stood up abruptly and offered his hand. Astonished by the unexpected consent, Charlie shook it automatically, stammered some thanks, and left, feeling suddenly committed and unsure of himself again.

A few days after the announcement of the forthcoming marriage had appeared in *The Times* and certain other newspapers, Charlie again sought out Louisa for a confidential interview in her parlour. He was looking unusually serious and quickly crushed her banter. From his pocket he drew out a document and placed it on her blotting pad.

'What's this?' she asked, recognising a legal document.

'It's a writ of Breach of Promise of Marriage, taken out against me by Irene Baker.'

'Irene? Crikey!'

'She's obviously seen the announcement in the papers. The twisting little bitch! Unless, of course…'

'No, Louisa. Absolutely not.'

'Well, you must admit you were a bit over the moon, there on the old Isle of Wight.'

'We had some fun, yes.'

'You sure you didn't get over-excited and drop a little hint? Give her a ring "just to remember you by"? Presents?'

'I gave her a lobster, if you call that a present.'

'What'd you give her that for?'

'To eat, of course.'

'Well, she can't bring that up in court. We hope.'

'Very funny. But it's not going to court. I've been with my lawyers half the day. They say if they get in touch with Irene's people the whole thing can be settled quietly, without anyone hearing a word of it.'

'Pay up, you mean?'

'Yes. They'll have to agree a sum of course.'

'But that's lettin' her win. Givin' in to bloody blackmail. Don't you do it, Charlie — or I'll never speak to you again.'

He said helplessly, 'But I can't face it in public. Think of the papers … the distress it'll cause everyone. You, too, Louisa. You and your hotel would be bound to be dragged in.'

She railed at him. 'All right, let me be dragged in. Let's all get dragged in. Charlie, you've got to face up to things in life. It's no good shovelling them under the carpet. Someone always finds 'em in the end. If you hush this up, and pay up, and one day your wife hears of it — which she will — then bang'll go your marriage, matey. She'll imagine all sort of other things you've been doing without letting on. She'll never trust you again.'

Charlie thought silently for some moments. Then he said miserably, 'I really don't think I can face Margaret and tell her about it.'

'You can face me, so why not her? You want to know how much she loves you — well, then, you'll find out this way.'

He considered this, then said with some relief, 'Oh hell, you're right as usual, I suppose.'

"Course I am. And it'll put old Sir Rosy to the test, too.'

It did, indeed, and he made no bones about his reaction. 'I am absolutely horrified by the whole business.'

'But James,' interceded Lord Henry Norton, in whom his nephew confided and who had accompanied him to see Sir James, 'Charlie had no idea. It came as a complete bolt from the blue. I mean to say, he's completely innocent, and if the marriage announcement hadn't appeared in the press this woman wouldn't have dreamed of trying it on.'

'You may think that, my dear Henry. You may indeed think that. But I was at the Bar as a young man, before I became a Member of Parliament, and I can tell you that these cases are very often — not to say usually — settled in an atmosphere of emotion. It is not like a ... a merchant overcharging for a ton of coal. Not at all. Who is acting for the plaintiff?'

'Some KC. Newsom, is it?'

'Newsom? Patrick Newsom? Good lord, he could blacken the character of the Archangel Gabriel and get damages from the Holy Ghost. Especially if the plaintiff were a pretty girl — which Irene Baker is. By the way, have you seen this?'

Sir James produced, with an air of distaste, a copy of that morning's *Daily Banner*, a newspaper which did not enter Lord Henry Norton's household, except to the downstairs region. The front page bore a large photograph of a young woman — Charlie recognised Irene Baker immediately — carefully posed, gazing wistfully at a framed photograph of himself.

'Monstrous!' Lord Henry exclaimed.

'You know what they say about love and war?' Sir James reminded him. 'I don't know whether word of this will have reached Margaret yet, but I intend to get her back to Dorset and do my best to soften the blow.'

'I should like to explain it to her myself,' Charlie said resolutely. Sir James shook his head.

'You've done enough harm to her for the moment, I think, Haslemere. I am not going to insist on a public announcement that the engagement is being cancelled. That would be tantamount to hitting a man when he's down. But if the case goes against you, I think you will know what honourable action to take.'

# CHAPTER ELEVEN

Despite Sir James Rosslyn's insistence, Charlie got to Margaret before her guardian could, and told her it all. To his intense relief, she responded by expressing complete belief in him.

She knew more of his reputation than he had even begun to suspect. Her guardian, it seemed, had dropped a few heavy hints when he had noticed them spending so much time together in Scotland. But she also had friends who knew Lord Haslemere in society and hadn't spared her the gossip. Her appearance of innocence of the world and its ways masked a good deal of shrewdness of judgement and capacity for broadmindedness. She had long since told herself that if Charles should ever propose to her, as she had for some time been expecting him to do, she would accept him, but must take him for what he had been and was. She imagined he would make a good husband for her, and a reliable father to her children, and would be faithful to her in his fashion. For more than that she did not hope. From the example of some of those friends of hers — the ones who were married — she had learned of the difference between willing companionship and the strain upon both parties of a possessive relationship.

So when Sir James at last came to her and requested her to pack her things and return to Dorset forthwith she declined politely, and when ordered, simply refused. There was nothing he could do to make her; in fact, he secretly admired her spirit The one thing he was adamant about, though, was that she should not receive newspaper reporters or attend the court. She consented to the former but argued about the latter. Only after Charles had seen her again, and added his plea to Sir James's, did she agree not to be present.

'But I'll have to sit here, in these wretched rooms, just waiting — not knowing,' she protested finally.

'You *do* know — don't you?' Charlie asked her gently. 'If you don't believe me, then no one's going to.'

'Oh, of course I do, darling!' she cried. 'I'm sorry. I know, when you come to tell me the news, it'll be good news. If there's any justice left in the world, that is.'

'I think you'll find there's a modicum of it about,' he smiled, and kissed her.

But even Charlie's confidence — and he was an optimist in most things — flagged a good deal in the awe-inspiring surroundings of the King's Bench Division of the High Court of Justice, with himself the centre of attention of several score people — barristers, ushers, policemen, clerks, pressmen, public, and a jury of twelve men, who from the look of them, might have been hand-picked as guardians of public morality. The only friendly faces he could discern were his uncle's and Louisa's. Sir James Rosslyn's expression was blank: he was plainly waiting to be convinced. Two or three of Charlie's female acquaintances were in the public seats. He would scarcely term them friends, though — just couriers for any juicy passages which might fail to get into print.

Irene Baker sat near her counsel. She was demurely dressed in a dark frock and hat, and looked wistfully ravishing. She gave Charlie a prolonged sweet smile, which achieved its purpose of being widely noticed. He returned a briefer one, and a polite little nod of acknowledgment.

When the elderly judge had taken his place and the opening formalities had been concluded, Irene's leading counsel, Newsom, a formidable looking being in comparison to

Charlie's own rather mousy man, Randall, proceeded to outline the plaintiff's case.

'For some years now my client, Miss Irene Baker, has enjoyed an increasingly successful career on the stage as an actress and dancer. She first met Lord Haslemere at a party at the Bentinck Hotel, Duke Street, early last year. Evidently they were mutually attracted, and Lord Haslemere took Miss Baker to supper at Romano's restaurant.

'The two parties continued to see each other from time to time, but their friendship can have said to have blossomed into something more intense during a holiday they both spent as guests of Mrs Trotter, the proprietress of the Bentinck Hotel, at her house on the Isle of Wight during August of last year.

'During that time Lord Haslemere proposed marriage to Miss Baker on several occasions, and later in London, but it was mutually agreed that no public announcement should be made until Lord Haslemere had had time to discuss the situation with his family and his trustees. Miss Baker also had contractual and other professional affairs to settle.

'At that time Lord Haslemere's ardour was such that he could hardly bear to be parted from Miss Baker for even a day or so — or, in his own words, "even an hour". When she was not with him he bombarded her with letters and telegrams.' Newsom picked up a small pile of papers from his desk and looked up at the judge. 'If I might be permitted to read out some extracts from these letters, M'lud?'

'If you consider them relevant,' the judge assented, to the obvious relief of the press and public.

'Regretfully, I do, M'lud.' Newsome selected one and began to read, '*My darling Pally…*'

'"Polly"? Who is this "Polly"?' the judge enquired.

175

'No, M'lud, "Pally",' counsel responded, to an accompaniment of subdued chuckles. '"Pally", M'lud, is Miss Baker. They called each other by pet names. Miss Baker was "Pally", Lord Haslemere "Ally" — derived, I am told, from the shortened name of a well-known London racecourse.'

There was open laughter at this, which an usher quelled. Charlie looked wretchedly down at his feet. Louisa seethed in her place. Irene Baker cast the jury a soulful glance.

Newsom continued to read. *'My darling Pally, I absolutely adore you, my love. Every hour away from you is agony. I am counting every* second *until Wednesday night. You are the most gloriously marvellous girl in the world…'*

Without seeming to do so, he was skilfully conveying to the jury the impression that here was a man of breeding and education so besotted with a woman that he had lapsed into the gushy sentiment of the cheapest romantic fiction. The reporters scribbled with a will as he went on.

'Another is dated August the ninth, 1909. *You are much the most important thing in my life… In returning my love you have paid me the greatest compliment possible… Every moment of the day and night I see your sweet face before me…'*

'September 20th, written from Lord Haslemere's house in Yorkshire: *How I shall miss you. I shall kiss your photograph every day. Please come back soon.* I should explain, M'lud, gentlemen of the jury, that Miss Baker was about to go away to Europe and South America for most of the winter on professional engagements. There are many more letters in a similar vein, but they tend, I am afraid, to become repetitive. If I might now call Miss Baker?'

With bowed head and shoulders sagging a little, Irene made her slow way to the witness stand. She began to read the oath so quietly that the judge had to request her to speak up. She did so with visible effort, but managed to swear firmly to tell nothing but the truth. Her voice, it was noted, was pleasant, though a trifle uncultivated for an actress.

'You may sit down, Miss Baker,' the judge told her in the tone he reserved exclusively for pretty female plaintiffs. She gave him a little bow and gratefully sat. Newsom turned to her, holding up a framed photograph — it was the one in the picture in the *Daily Banner*.

'Miss Baker, did Lord Haslemere send you this photograph of himself?'

'He did. And I sent him one of myself with a similar inscription.'

'Will you kindly read that inscription?'

With just the hint of a break in her voice, Irene read out, '*To my adorable Pally, with my everlasting love.*'

Newsom put down the photograph. 'Lord Haslemere suggested marriage to you on a number of occasions?' he asked.

'Yes.'

'Can you remember his exact words?'

'N-no. Not now.' This time her voice almost did break. 'I was … so much in love myself…'

Newsom consulted one of the letters again. '*In returning my love you have paid me the greatest compliment possible.* How did you interpret those words, written to you in a letter early in August?'

'Well, I thought they just confirmed what I already knew — that Lord Haslemere wished to marry me.'

The judge intervened at this point, addressing Newsom. 'I cannot detect any firm proposal of marriage in those words myself, Mr Newsom. Is there such a proposal in any of the letters before you?'

'Not as such, M'lud. There are many inferences to be drawn, however...'

'And it is right and proper that it should be the jury who should draw them, Mr Newsom.'

'As your lordship pleases.'

Newsom sat down and Charlie's counsel got up. Charlie did not know him, but he had been highly recommended by Sir James Rosslyn. He was discouragingly unprepossessing.

'Miss Baker,' he addressed her in a flat tone, 'we have heard that you and Lord Haslemere formed a ... a warm friendship during a holiday by the seaside last summer. You assert that he offered you his hand in marriage. Did he give you any more tangible tokens of his love? Any presents, for instance?'

The lobster was either forgotten or ignored. Irene replied, 'I didn't want any. He was all I wanted.'

'And no engagement ring?'

'We decided it would be best for me professionally if he only gave me the ring when we put the engagement in the papers.'

'I see,' Randall nodded. 'So you waited, worried yet patient. You waited, in fact, until the end of May of this year when Lord Haslemere did announce his engagement in the newspapers — but to another lady.'

'Yes, sir.'

'How did you hear of his engagement to Miss Wormald?'

'I saw it in the papers.'

'Ah, of course. Yet ... you didn't write to him? You just issued him with a writ of Breach of Promise of Marriage?'

'I was too upset. I was really ill. Too ill to work.' Irene threw the jury a despairing look. 'It ... it has ruined my life.'

'And yet,' Randall insisted, with a spark of animation which surprised Charlie and raised a flicker of hope in him, 'and yet you were able to give an interview to the press, and have your photograph taken holding his photograph — within the same week?'

'Well, they wanted it…'

'Don't you think that was rather a cruel thing to do?' he pressed on, ignoring her response. 'Cruel not only to him, but to the lady he had become engaged to?'

Irene flushed and retorted, 'It was him was being cruel to me. That's all I thought.'

'I see. And yet, all through the winter and the early spring of this year you never wrote one word to Lord Haslemere?'

'Well, I was busy … travelling round all over the place.'

'Weren't you worried that he never wrote to you?'

'Of course I was. But men don't like girls that push. And I had his promise, and his photo. And I knew — well, I thought I knew, he'd be kissing it every day and remembering me, like he'd said he would.' Her voice began to go again, and there was a murmur in court as a tear was seen to glisten on each of her cheeks as she managed to say, 'I had his promise — as a gentleman,' before she broke down completely.

'Randall didn't sound awfully hopeful afterwards,' Charlie told Louisa. They were seated that night in her parlour, sipping the inevitable champagne, which was doing nothing to elevate their spirits.

'He's a bit of a drip, if you ask me,' she said. 'He didn't put up any sort of fight. As for that girl and her play-acting — ugh! Enough to make you sick.'

Charlie nodded gloomy agreement. 'I'm sure it isn't affecting the jury that way, though. Old Sir James said these cases are often decided on sentiment, or whatever you call it. You know — the wicked young rake and the poor injured actress…'

'It's the rich wot gets the pleasure…'

Charlie finished his glass and declined a refill. 'I'm afraid Margaret's going to be most dreadfully upset,' were his last words, as he went off to his rooms and a much-needed sleep.

Louisa sat for a while, deep in thought. Then she opened the door and bellowed for Merriman. The waiter came out from the dispense and was pushed into her room and the door shut behind him.

'You're coming to court with me tomorrow,' Louisa told him without preamble. 'So try to tidy yourself up a bit. You look like a walkin' scarecrow.'

'Oh, not me, ma'am. Not in any court. I … I wouldn't know what to say.'

'You'll be asked questions and you'll answer them.'

'Mixed up in a court of law!' he was mumbling on. 'No good for a hotel, madam. Nothing turns the guests away like —'

'Shut up when I'm talking! Lord Haslemere's in the tripe, and we got to help get him out of it the best way we can. If it wasn't for him, we wouldn't be here now, healthy and happy. There wouldn't even be no Bentinck, an' you'd have gone to your last rest years ago. He pulled us out of it when we was in it, so we're goin' to do the same for him. Right?'

The old man had no option but to consent.

'Lord Haslemere,' Newsom addressed Charlie next morning, 'are you in all honesty, and under oath, prepared to say to this court that you never, at any time, thought for a moment of proposing marriage to Miss Baker?'

'Yes … or I should say no,' Charlie replied with a confusion which kindled a special sort of gleam in his antagonist's eye. 'I really never seriously gave it a thought.'

'Yet we have heard that in writing you several times pledged your eternal love for Miss Baker, whom you referred to constantly as adorable, incredibly lovely, et cetera, et cetera.'

Charlie shuffled to his feet and looked appealingly towards the judge, who was writing notes and ignored him. 'I know I did,' he admitted. 'It sounds rather silly ... especially when read out ... but you see, at the time ... last summer ... I was rather struck with her.'

Now the judge was looking at him keenly, as Newsom suggested, 'Infatuated?'

'Well, yes, I suppose so. We were having a lot of fun together ... and she was rather keen on me. In fact, she wrote a lot of the same sort of nonsense to me. I burnt her letters. I think that's the best thing to do with, well, private letters.'

'That sort of "nonsense" — as you are pleased to call it so casually, nearly a year later — can be rather serious, Lord Haslemere. Enough to break a girl's heart. Having toyed with Miss Baker's affections, you just casually went away and left her hoping ... waiting...' He emphasised his words with an airy flutter of the fingers of his right hand.

'Oh, not exactly,' Charlie protested mildly. 'I mean, we had dinner together in London. I think it was in September. She seemed in very good form, chattering about her dancing and all that sort of thing. But things had, well, rather cooled off between us by then — or I thought they had.'

'The onset of winter, no doubt,' remarked the judge and received his deferential laugh from all round the court. Randall, Sir James, Lord Henry and Louisa Trotter were not smiling, though. Neither was Merriman, seated at Louisa's side and looking thoroughly apprehensive.

'Quite honestly,' Charlie blurted out without having been questioned, 'I just wish Irene ... Miss Baker ... had written to me. The last thing I'd have wanted would have been to distress her — in any way. If I'd only…'

He looked about him desperately. His counsel was looking more mournful than ever, playing with his pencil. Louisa's eyes were blazing at Charlie, telling him to shut his silly mouth. He got the message and obeyed.

Then it was Louisa's turn to take the witness stand, to the keen interest of the onlookers. Since she was a defence witness it was the mousy Randall who questioned her first.

'Mrs Trotter, you have known Lord Haslemere very well for some considerable time?'

'That's right,' she answered confidently. 'He's been a resident in my hotel for must be nearly ten years. And he's a great personal friend of mine, as you might say.'

'Do you think Lord Haslemere is the sort of person who would propose marriage to a lady and then, er, leave her in the lurch?'

Despite an objection from Newsom to this mode of questioning, Louisa answered and the judge let her do so.

'It isn't what I *think*. I *know* he wouldn't. Lord Haslemere's a gentleman and he knows how to treat ladies. And I don't mean just ladies, I mean women of all sorts. He'd be just as nice and polite and thoughtful to the old girl who sells matches outside in Duke Street as he is to everyone else. He's the most thoughtful, kind-hearted, decent man I've ever had the pleasure of meeting … and I know men.'

Someone in the public seats guffawed at this and was promptly shut up by a withering stare from Louisa.

'What's more, me lord,' she told the judge, 'Lord Haslemere's just the sort of nice bloke that a certain sort of woman always takes advantage of. And there's one other thing I can tell you.

Lord Haslemere wouldn't never ask a girl to marry him — not without consulting me first.'

The judge raised his eyebrows. 'Lord Haslemere became engaged recently. Did he consult you first in that case?'

'Yes, me lord. He certainly did.'

'Thank you, Mrs Trotter,' said Randall, and sat down, pleased with the beneficial effect the judge had produced for him. Newsom was quickly on to his feet to try to reverse it.

'Mrs Trotter,' he beamed, deceptively amiably, 'if I may say so, you seem to be a woman of some considerable character.'

Louisa was unimpressed by the flattery, but said, 'If that's a compliment, I accept it.'

'It is indeed, madam. Now, you also know the plaintiff in this case well, I believe?'

'If you mean Irene Baker, not half as well as I thought I did.'

'Lord Haslemere and Miss Baker first met in your hotel — under your auspices?'

'Yes. There was a little party going on, and I introduced them.'

'How very pleasant of you. And later you asked Lord Haslemere and Miss Baker to stay with you for a holiday at your house on the Isle of Wight?'

'Well? What's wrong with that?'

'Nothing. Nothing at all. Only, it might seem to some people that perhaps you were deliberately throwing the two together. Matchmaking, possibly?'

'They were my friends and I just wanted us all to have a nice bit of a holiday together.'

'But it got rather out of hand?'

'They fell for each other, if that's what you mean.'

Newsom asked, a shade more sharply, looking at the jury as he did so, 'You admit that, in your opinion, they fell in love?'

'Boys do fall in love with pretty dancers.'

'Lord Haslemere is hardly a boy.'

'Well, he is to me. Anyway, it was only a bit of fun.'

Newsom turned back to face her. His tone was perceptibly hardening now, and he no longer smiled. 'You have heard some of the contents of Lord Haslemere's letters. I should have thought "infatuation" would be a better word than "fun".'

'All right, then. Use it if you want to,' Louisa retorted to some chuckles. 'It's the same thing, though, and if people can't write that sort of nonsense to each other, then the world would be a pretty dull old place. Though I do say,' she added to the judge, 'me own motto is "No letters, no lawyers, and kiss me baby's bottom."'

'An admirable sentiment and excellent advice,' agreed the judge, who had seen too many men come adrift in his courts through having put pen to paper. As if sensing that Louisa was winning the sympathy of the judge and perhaps the jury for the defendant, Newsom persisted with his questioning.

'As they were staying with you, Mrs Trotter, no doubt you were in an ideal position to observe their conduct towards one another?'

'Oh, yeh.' Louisa leaned across the stand and gave the barrister her winning smile. 'Look, sir — you're a nice-looking gentleman. No doubt you've had a cuddle and a kiss with girls in your time…'

The court rocked with laughter. The judge found it necessary to blow his nose with a handkerchief fortunately big enough to conceal his lips. An usher restored some semblance of order, but to the general delight, and the obvious embarrassment of Newsom, Louisa was going on imperviously.

'Every time you took a girl in your arms and kissed her, and whispered sweet nothin's in her ear, you didn't think she was thinkin' you was askin' her to marry you, did you?'

When order had been restored again, Louisa concluded, standing up straight now, her smile gone and her face turned towards the jury, 'Well, Irene Baker didn't, neither. When she saw that engagement in the papers, she thought she'd have a go, knowing Charlie Haslemere's as soft as butter when it comes to bloody women. She's just out to squeeze a bit of cash out of him, that's all.'

'M'lud, I object most strongly,' Newsom cried, but Louisa shouted him down.

'Then when Lord Haslemere didn't come up to scratch right away, the poor, lovelorn girl asks a photographer from the papers to come and take a picture of her mopin' over her lost lover. My heart bleeds for her, it does. I tell you this, by the time she saw that engagement notice she'd got so many other irons in the fire she'd almost forgotten about Lord Haslemere. She…'

Something like chaos reigned briefly, with Newsom objecting, Randall bleating to Louisa to be quiet, the judge ordering her to be silent, and the usher vainly trying to control the spectators. At last, under combined efforts, order was restored. The judge, who had given Louisa an inch and regretfully seen her take a yard, told her sternly, 'Mrs Trotter, if you do not stop uttering these unsupported calumnies against the plaintiff, it will be my duty to have you removed from this court by force, or even arrested for contempt.'

Louisa answered quietly and respectfully, 'I'm sorry, me lord. I ain't got contempt for no one in this court — only for her.' She nodded towards Irene Baker, who sat pale with fury and alarm.

Newsom was glad to get rid of Louisa, and Randall, desperately needing to silence her before she could undo all the good she seemed to have done, said he had no more questions for her. The judge dismissed her from the stand with some relief, but a certain amount of regret. His court was by no means often so lively.

Her place at the witness stand was taken by an old man, every inch still the Victorian. He agreed with the clerk that his name was Arthur Cornelius Merriman.

Randall asked him, 'Are you a waiter employed at the Bentinck Hotel in Duke Street?'

'I am the head waiter, sir,' Merriman answered with dignity. 'Have been since —'

'Yes, yes. Do you recognise the plaintiff?'

'Who?'

'That lady, sitting there.'

'Oh, Miss Baker — yes. Yes, I do indeed.'

'Have you seen that lady on the premises of the Bentinck Hotel at any time during the last six months?'

Newsom's head jerked up sharply when he heard this. He frowned and looked across at his client as Merriman replied, 'Yes, sir.'

The old man took out a pair of spectacles which might have been as old as himself and put them on. He produced a little red exercise book and turned to a marked page. *December 12th,'* he read out. *'Spent the night in No. 11.'*

The judge said, 'I don't understand. You mean she took a room — number eleven?'

'No, my lord. It was a gentleman who had the room.'

A loud murmur quickly died away as the judge went on to ask, 'How do you know Miss Baker spent the night in this room with this gentleman?'

'Because, me lord, she was there last thing, when I took them their drinks, and she was still there next morning, when I took them their breakfast.' Without waiting for any response to this he turned pages of his notebook and read again, *'January 7th and 16th in No. 8…'*

'One moment,' the judge interrupted him. He turned to address Newsom, who rose to his feet.

'Mr Newsom, I believe your client said in evidence that she was out of the country during the winter months.'

Newsom had a quick, whispered consultation with Irene, then told the judge, 'Not all the winter months, M'lud.'

'Evidently. Pray proceed, Mr Randall.' But Randall left Merriman to continue with yet another extract from his surprise chronicle.

*'On January 24th the young lady entered the hotel with the Marquis of—'*

Randall stopped him urgently. 'No names, please, Mr Merriman. It will be sufficient if you will refer to the noble lord as Lord X.'

Merriman cupped his ear with his obtuse gesture. 'Lord who?'

'Lord X.'

The old head was shaken. 'I never heard of any Lord Hexe, sir, and I take pride there's not many I don't —'

'Thank you. Thank you, Mr Merriman. That will be all,' Charlie's counsel said, fearing to tread further.

Unseen by any of the principals in the case, a woman had quietly entered the court and slipped into one of the few vacant seats. All eyes were on Newsom as he rose to glare challengingly at Merriman. His voice was acid with sarcasm.

'Mr Merriman, are your duties as waiter — I beg your pardon, *head* waiter — at the Bentinck Hotel arduous?'

'I should just say so, sir. On me feet all day and half the night…'

'Yet you seem to find ample time to play the detective as well.'

'Part of the job, I've always reckoned, sir.' He flourished the exercise book. 'Keep a note of who comes and goes — what they like and don't like. Who shouldn't know who's been with who, if anyone asks, if you get my drift?'

Newsom's voice was louder this time as he turned to face the jury again, saying to Merriman, 'In that case, Mr Detective Merriman, I put it to you that your researches will have served to convince his lordship and the jury that the Bentinck Hotel is nothing more than a common house of assignation.'

The court was hushed, with all eyes on Merriman. Newsom, too, had swivelled round dramatically on his last words to face him. The old man was not to be flustered, though. He answered quietly, 'Not at all, sir. Mrs Trotter won't allow no ladies of the town in the hotel, sir. No streetwalkers. Very strict rule, that. She likes her guests to be free and easy, like they was in their own homes, as you might say.'

Newsom hesitated. All the arrogance of complete confidence had left him. Suddenly, there seemed to be no line of questioning he could pursue with safety. He mumbled something and sat down.

A piece of paper, scribbled on by the woman who had so recently entered the court, had been passed down to Randall. He turned to look at her, and Louisa and Charlie followed his surprised gaze. They saw that she was Margaret Wormald. Randall glanced at them, then rose.

'My Lord,' he addressed the judge, who was writing savagely, 'Lord Haslemere's fiancée, Miss Margaret Wormald, is in court and has expressed her willingness to come forward and give evidence.'

The judge tossed his pen down. 'I am sure Miss Wormald's gesture is an admirable one,' he said. 'But apart from the fact that she is in no position to give any evidence which might have bearing on this matter, and might only succeed unwittingly in inflicting further pain on herself and Lord Haslemere — quite apart from these considerations, I have had enough of this most impertinent and disgusting case, which in my opinion should never have been brought. Gentlemen of the jury, I instruct you to find for the defendant, Lord Haslemere. The plaintiff will pay all costs.'

He got up and, after the most perfunctory of bows, swept out.

'The court is adjourned,' the clerk called. 'Clear the court.'

No one heard him. The hubbub of delight was too great.

# CHAPTER TWELVE

The wedding took place several weeks later, on a fine September day. Louisa attended. At first she had wanted to decline the invitation, but then had made herself accept. Merriman, too, had been there, as a reward for his vital part in the court case.

Mary Philips and Starr were left in charge of the hotel, Major Smith-Barton being away. It was a hectic time. The publicity which the case had attracted had certainly had no adverse effect on the Bentinck's reputation. Quite the opposite, in fact. Every apartment and room was taken and applicants were having to be turned away. Only one apartment stood vacant, and that, too, had been prepared for the arrival of occupants — Lord and Lady Haslemere, who were to spend the first night of their marriage in Charlie's suite before leaving for the Continent.

'Everything all right, Starr?' Louisa asked the overworked porter when she returned that evening, dressed in her wedding finery. 'The Haslemeres' rooms all ready?'

'Yes, madam. Mary attended to them personally.'

'Well, I'll just go up and take a look myself.'

She went. Merriman, who had shared the wedding car with her, came in looking remarkably dapper and sporting a carnation in his buttonhole.

'Oh, good evening, my lord,' Starr greeted him. 'Fred, get out of that basket and give his lordship a bow? Fred merely yawned. 'How was the wedding?' Starr asked his colleague.

'Very pleasant. Reception wasn't up to much, though. Food very badly done and wine undrinkable. Should've had it here.'

'No thanks! There's enough doing without that. Your temporary's useless, by the way. Half sozzled, I reckon. The sooner you're into your harness, the better.'

Merriman groaned resignedly and wandered off to the dispense to change and get back to work.

In Charlie's rooms Louisa automatically checked the flowers, the perfectly laid dining table, the position of the cushions. Mary had done her job with her usual thoroughness.

Louisa's eye fell on the bottle of champagne, already chilling in the ice bucket. It was Clicquot Rose '93, the very wine she and Charlie had drunk in these same surroundings on the evening they had fallen in love. The sight of it stirred sharp recollections in her: the echo of their abandonedly singing 'And Her Golden Hair Was Hanging Down Her Back', to Charlie's inept piano accompaniment; their charged conversation, which had begun with her chaffing him about the amorous approaches he would have made to the woman who should have been dining with him, but whose defection had led to Louisa's taking her place.

*'Then I tell her that I love her.'*

*'And the magic spell always works?'*

*'No… Sometimes the lady says her carriage is waiting.'*

And after the long pause, her own words: *'I haven't got a carriage.'*

She was brought back from this reverie by voices and movement at the door. Charlie and Margaret came in, followed by Starr with Margaret's luggage. Louisa braced herself and greeted them.

'Welcome. Welcome home. I hope you'll be comfortable, Lady Haslemere.'

'Margaret, please, Louisa. Unless you're going to start calling Charles "Lord".'

'Not likely,' was the instant response. 'I can think of some other things to call him at times, but Charlie'd be safer.'

They both kissed her and she left them to it, going down to her parlour without troubling to change her clothes and busying herself at once with accumulated paperwork. It was quite late when Merriman came in with a tray bearing a bottle of champagne in an ice bucket and two glasses. She saw from the label that it was Clicquot Rosé again.

'Here, what's this?' she demanded. 'I never ordered…'

'I did,' Charlie said, entering past the waiter. 'Margaret's having a rest before supper, so I thought perhaps…'

'Good idea!' Louisa said, with real pleasure. 'Pink champagne. Didn't even know we had any left in the cellar.' She suddenly recalled using these same words on that same evening years ago.

Charlie recalled them, too, and repeated his reply: 'Merriman and I knew … didn't we, Merriman?'

'The last bottle of the '93, madam,' the old man answered. He opened it, poured and withdrew, closing the door.

'Old muddleman,' Louisa grinned. 'He was tickled pink you asked him to the wedding. I don't reckon he's ever been to one where he was served instead of serving. Poor old Starr's real put out, I reckon.'

'Well, I couldn't invite a damn dog as well, could I?'

They laughed, but there was an uneasiness between them.

Louisa said, 'It was a nice wedding. Your … Margaret made a lovely bride.'

'I thought old Sir James's speech was going on for ever…'

'Oh, well, he was paying, wasn't he? And he likes the sound of his own voice.'

Charlie poured out some more champagne and carried Louisa's glass to where she still sat at her desk. He hesitated, then sat down on his own chair again and said, 'Louisa … I think probably this will be the last night I shall spend in the Bentinck.'

The tension she had been conscious of was released in a bristling retort. 'Oh, is it? She's worked pretty quick, hasn't she? I might have guessed. Hardly gets you to the altar before she starts…'

He said gently, 'It's nothing to do with Margaret. She doesn't even know about it. But, you see, we'll need somewhere to live in London, and a hotel isn't, well, a very suitable place to begin married life.'

'I don't see why not. Anyway, Lady … Margaret will mostly be in Yorkshire, won't she? I'd have thought she'd been glad to have no domestic worries for you, and food provided. Seems an ideal arrangement to me.'

Charlie took a deep breath. He had had to summon up all his resources of courage for this interview. 'Louisa, my darling,' he said, 'it won't do. You've got to let me go. It's no good trying to hold on.'

'I dunno what you're talkin' about,' she said, but she spoke automatically, knowing full well.

He explained, 'You once said to me that we've got to be honest with ourselves. Not to pull the wool. Well, let's be honest now. If my marriage is to have any hope it's got to be without your help.'

'I don't own you.'

'You do, really. You have done for the past seven or eight years. I've come to rely on you completely, and you've never let me down. I even had to ask you if I ought to marry Margaret at all. Well, now I've got to learn the lessons you've tried to teach me. Learn to walk on my own two feet — to be responsible for my wife and … children…'

Louisa sighed. 'Yeh,' she said after some moments. 'All right.' She paused again, then said, 'I didn't really ought to ask you this, Charlie … but it may be my last chance for a bit. Have you seen our little girl?'

'Oh, yes. I saw her last Christmas. We have a sort of party for all the tenants' children on the estate. She's bright as a bee. The schoolmistress has had to invent a special class for her. And she's going to be a beauty.'

'Well, that's not a bad start in life — depending on how things turn out.'

'Louisa,' Charlie went on, coming to the other difficult part of what he had to say, 'I'm going to leave my money in the hotel.'

She shook her head, as he had foreseen she would. 'You don't have to. It isn't a charity.'

'That's nothing to do with it. I happen to regard it as a very good investment. And I want you to have the furniture that's in my rooms, in part payment of a debt, which, whatever I did, I could never repay you in full.'

'Nonsense!' was her immediate reaction. But then she said, seeing that her refusal would hurt him, 'Oh well, thanks.'

She stood up. He did, too, and went to stand looking down into her huge blue eyes. 'Whatever happens to us, Louisa darling,' he said, 'I want you to know that some part of me will always be yours alone.'

He drew her to him and kissed her long and tenderly. She responded almost desperately, as if it were the last thing that was going to happen in her life. Then he released her suddenly and went quickly from the room.

Left by herself, in the late evening gloom, Louisa felt lonelier and sadder than she could remember having felt ever. She idly picked up the champagne bottle. It was empty. She upended it and stuck it neck first into the ice bucket. The finality of the gesture jerked her out of her mood.

'Men!' she said out loud to the room — and went back to her papers.

# ACKNOWLEDGEMENTS

This novel is based on episodes in the BBC Television serial *The Duchess of Duke Street* and is a sequel to one similarly based, *The Way Up*. The author wishes to thank the BBC and John Hawkesworth, creator and producer of the serial, for their kind co-operation, and to acknowledge that in writing this book she has drawn upon material by the following scriptwriters:

JULIAN BOND
BILL CRAIG
JOHN HAWKESWORTH
JEREMY PAUL

# A NOTE TO THE READER

If you have enjoyed this novel enough to leave a review on **Amazon** and **Goodreads**, then we would be truly grateful.

Sapere Books

**Sapere Books** is an exciting new publisher of brilliant fiction and popular history.

To find out more about our latest releases and our monthly bargain books visit our website:
**saperebooks.com**

Printed in Great Britain
by Amazon

38519826R00116